Bad Faith

Bad Faith

Gillian Philip

www.stridentpublishing.co.uk

Published by
Strident Publishing Ltd
22 Strathwhillan Drive
The Orchard, Hairmyres
East Kilbride G75 8GT

Tel: +44 (0)1355 220588
info@stridentpublishing.co.uk
www.stridentpublishing.co.uk

A catalogue record for this book is
available from the British Library.

ISBN 978-1-905537-08-2

Typeset in Optima
Designed by Sallie Moffat
Cover image © the earlybird, 2008
Printed by Creative Print and Design

Gillian Philip was born in Glasgow and has been writing all her life, starting with short but frenetic novels about Captain Scarlet and The Man From UNCLE (having massive crushes on both). She has worked as a barmaid, theatre usherette, record store assistant, radio presenter, typesetter, and political assistant to a parliamentary candidate. While living in Barbados, where her steadiest job was as a singer in an Irish bar, she took up writing professionally, and wrote many short stories for women's magazines. In 2001 she moved back to Scotland, and now lives in Morayshire with husband Ian, twins Lucy and Jamie, and Oscar, the fastest terrier in the west.

For

Jamie and Lucy
and for my dad, Bob Allsopp

Thank you...

Hilary Johnson, for endless help and encouragement; Lin Anderson, for restoring my faith in Bad Faith; Alison Boyle and Sarah Molloy, for great advice on the manuscript; Kate Pool at the Society of Authors, for answering legal questions; the Rt Revd Mark Strange, for reading my manuscript and not minding when I stole his cheese; all writing buddies, especially Maggie Craig, Elizabeth Garrett, Linda Gillard, Michael 'Mad Dog' Malone and Elizabeth Ramsey; Frances Smith; Keith Charters, Graham Watson, Alison Stroak and Sallie Moffat at Strident, for everything; Susan Sloan for her wonderful cover illustrations; Cherry Allsopp, Derek Allsopp...

And Ian, Lucy and Jamie – for putting up with a wife and mother who is more often than not away with the faeries.

A little water clears us of this deed

Macbeth

It Ain't Necessarily So

Ira Gershwin

Dystopia (n): an imaginary place that is
depressingly wretched

The Penguin English Dictionary

Before

Before I slipped on the mud and fell over the Bishop, our family didn't have a lot to do with murder.

A little, but not much.

There was Holy Joe, of course, and that family legend about the narrow escape of Aunt Abby's best friend's boyfriend's sister, but that's another story.

Though not entirely.

Holy Joe stopped killing women about twenty years ago and was never heard of again. Perhaps he thought he'd done his bit for the morality of the nation, though heaven knows what the poor throttled women felt about that, since none of them had done more than leave a dance late, or give a boyfriend a seriously mistimed goodnight smooch. You might call Holy Joe a serial killer; the religious militias called him a folk hero. He was doing the One God's work. Rumour said he was a high-ranking militia member himself. Maybe that's why the police didn't exactly fall over themselves to find the old psycho.

That was my Dad's theory, anyway.

You might also think the militias would disband when they got their way and their God-fearing religious state. Well, it turns out that telling everyone what to do, and shooting them in the kneecaps when they don't oblige, is way too much fun to give up just because you get what you say you want. So the militias went on defending the nation's morals and generally having a rare old time and

I daresay nobody liked to ask them to stop, least of all the One Church.

That was my brother's theory.

You can tell from all this how much ear-bending I have to put up with at home. Personally, I don't give politics a lot of thought. Be modest and pious and keep your mouth shut, that's my motto. I suppose I love my country, and I like a peaceful life, and there's not much crime, apart from political crime and an occasional morality offence. (I'm not counting the militias. After all, the police don't.) Women have rights like anyone else: when anyone complains (and they tend not to), the One Church only has to point to Ma Baxter, President, First Minister and Mother of the Nation. And militias or no militias, at least us girls don't have to worry about Holy Joe any more. Not that we ever did, if we were good and holy and kept our hands and bodies and opinions to ourselves. Holy Joe stopped his killing because the nation stopped being godless.

And that was my grandmother's theory, when she was alive.

Two years ago she was only just alive, flat out in a hospital room that smelt of Pine-Sol, dead dahlias and pee, and for some reason I thought about her Holy Joe theories as I sat by her deathbed. I felt depressed because the place and the smell were so familiar and I'd spent way too long in here myself, that time I was incredibly stupid and didn't look where I was going and ran in front of a car. I really hated dahlias, having got mightily sick of them when I was stuck in this same private room with a splintered pelvis and a fractured skull, so that's why I hadn't got Bunty a fresh bunch even though I should have. To make up for it I was holding onto her hand the way you're expected to, the way I've seen it done on TV soaps like *Angels and Martyrs*, only I was beginning to wonder if Bunty was planning on taking me with her. Her grip was that strong. Since I was only thirteen at the time, I had no intention of tagging along.

They say old people don't want to linger, but not Bunty. Bunty intended to linger indefinitely. I sat there holding onto her hand, feeling sorry for her but a little uncomfortable too – we weren't really a hand-holding family – and I kept hoping Mum or Dad would come back and give me a break. My grandmother was trying to say something, and I dreaded that she might manage. I didn't want her last words to me to be *You look like a boy, Cassandra, grow your hair!* Or *You get your scrawny behind into Church tonight or I'll be leathering it for you.* Or *Why aren't you taller, look at the height of me!*

Well, she'd shrunk a bit now, marginally reducing her power to terrify, and whatever she wanted to tell me would have to wait for the afterlife, because my grandmother had lost the power of speech. She had not lost the power of her fingers. She hung onto mine like grim death – and I know that's a tactless way to put it, since that was just what she was trying to avoid. But she did not want to slip peacefully away. She did not want to slip away *at all.*

Well, if you've been fighting the world your whole life like Bunty did, fighting to keep your family fed and clothed, and then just fighting your family afterwards because it had become a bit of a habit, maybe you're bound to fight the end of it. Her rheumy eyes were locked on mine and I could almost hear her yelling in my head, *Don't you let me go, Cassie! Don't you dare!* Bunty was hanging onto life by her gnarled fingernails the way she always had, and she wasn't about to let go now, which meant my hand was starting to turn blue.

In the end I did get my circulation back, because of course Bunty could not hold on like that forever. She died anyway. Not on my watch. She died while I was out of the room, and I still reckon she was so annoyed with me for prising her fingers off, she did it out of spite.

Only afterwards, when I'd stopped being ashamed and slightly embarrassed, and started being sorry she was dead, did I realise she was scared to die. She was hanging on not out of habit but because she was petrified. I wondered what exactly she was petrified of, and I suppose I could have asked my father, but the way things turned out, I'm glad I didn't. I was always nervous of asking these great theological questions anyway, in case I was supposed to know the answer already and just hadn't been paying attention in school. (Which I hadn't.)

Well, Bunty had been dead ancient, and now she was just dead. Dad took the funeral, of course, despite his life-long hatred of Elvis Presley. I don't think Bunty was that keen on him either, but Aunt Abby was a big fan, and Aunt Abby chose the music. Elvis hadn't been banned by then, so Bunty was sent off to the strains of How Great Thou Art. Should have been *Please, Don't Release Me. Oh, Please Don't Let Me Go.*

Beneath the Elvis CD you could just hear the electric hum of the conveyor belt taking Bunty to meet her probably apprehensive Maker. When the pleated curtain came down to swallow her, the music stopped and you could hear Dad intoning something reassuring and pious, which is his job. And right then, as I was looking at him and wondering if he knew just how much Bunty had wanted *not* to Go Forth Upon Her Journey From The World, I saw him look at Mum, and then I saw Mum look at Aunt Abby.

They were not exchanging the look that meant *Aw, it was a release poor soul, it was how she'd have wanted it.* They just looked enormously relieved, as if to say *That's that, then*.

Out of nowhere I thought again about Aunt Abby's best friend's boyfriend's sister and her famously narrow escape. If that was what it was, since nobody could be sure it was Holy Joe who walked her home. Maybe it was some other black-haired limping pale-eyed man with a scar above his eyebrow. I suppose there might have been two like that in a city the size of Bunty's.

It was odd, but I knew, as Dad and Mum and Aunt Abby crossed themselves hurriedly, that they were thinking about Holy Joe too.

Then we were all standing in line to be kissed by damp and weepy friends and neighbours, a lot of whom would be going the same way as Bunty in the not-too-distant future, and they knew it. Which was a big part of why they were sad.

And I thought the same as Mum and Dad and Abby: *That's that, then*.

But as it turned out? It wasn't.

1: Graphic Violence

Up in his disgusting pit of a room, my brother was brutally murdering an innocent nun.

'How's it going?' I ventured.

'Fine,' he said. 'Level one.'

'*Still?*'

'Go away.'

One toe in the door, one eye open, I watched. These black market games could be stomach-churningly realistic, even trash like *Hell Breaker II*. I made a show of turning my face away, but I was as riveted as I was repelled.

Level One. Jeez. Griff was not very good at computer games, lacking both dexterity and focus. I like to think he also lacked ruthlessness, but I'm less sure about that now.

Besides, he was quite often trying to play with one hand. His console sat on his desk, his desk sat right by the open sash window, and his left hand was usually hanging out of it. He was not fooling anybody, of course. You could smell the cigarette smoke a mile off, but he liked to think he was fooling the parents.

My brother started out as a chubby and adorable blond baby (I'm told), became a chubby adorable toddler and then a lanky adorable fair-haired child, at all stages capable of sending maiden aunts into paroxysms of love (even Aunt Abby, who Dad said was no maiden).

When puberty hit, he turned overnight into Gothic Grim Griffin. His hair went dark. His taste in music went dark.

His long night of the soul went dark. The broody Young Byron look was somewhat spoiled by the rash of acne on his chin, but maybe Young Byron had plooks too.

Now I said, 'Guess what?'

'No,' said Griff, decapitating a demon of the sixth circle.

'No, really. Okay, don't guess, I'll tell you.'

He sighed. He must have got decapitated right back, because he relaxed in his swivel chair and folded his arms, brought the cigarette indoors for a suck, and blew the smoke out into the blue sky. 'Go on then. And go away after that.'

'Bishop Todd's gone missing,' I said.

It was a bit of a strain to put the right amount of concern and sadness into my voice. Bishop Todd was popular, jolly and pious and stout, but nobody can deny it is lovely being first with Breaking News. I could almost see the strap of text running along the bottom of the imaginary screen in front of me. *Bishop Todd Goes Missing.*

'No. Has he really?' Griff's tone was on the sarcastic side.

'Yes, really.' *Bishop Todd Really Goes Missing.* 'He never came back from a walk yesterday. They've had helicopters out.'

Griff rolled his eyes. 'I'm surprised they haven't got the army out.'

'They have,' I told him smugly. *Army Joins Bishop Todd Search.*

'Really?' Now he did sound impressed. 'The Army? So, really missing, eh?'

'Uh-huh. Well, a bit of the army,' I admitted. 'Ma Baxter was on TV, expressing the nation's deep concern. Dabbing her eyes with a hankie, the works.'

That wasn't surprising. Bishop Todd was big pals with the Mother of the Nation, and he was her Spiritual Adviser too, which gave him more power than her Vice President and her Finance Minister put together. He'd been one of the first to abandon his sect and join the One Church, as soon as he saw which way the political wind was blowing. He'd been loudest in denouncing doubters, and fiercest in defending the militias. ('Their methods may be misguided, but the anger of these young people is righteous and their motives are holy.' I knew that quote off by heart because you saw the edited version on a thousand t-shirts, printed beneath a portrait of the Bishop: *Our anger is righteous, our motives are holy*.)

At any rate, he'd raced up the One Church hierarchy like a demented squirrel. He'd kept his home in a very posh part of our suburb, and sometimes we saw him, striding around rather pompously in his cassock and pressing the flesh of the Faithful. (He didn't need bodyguards. Nobody would ever dare mug the Bishop.) Most of his time, though, was spent in the heart of the capital, lurking at the seat of power and giving spiritual guidance to Ma Baxter. The rumour was he'd be her Religious Security Minister within six months, and then the rest of the Cabinet might as well stay home and knit. Oh yes, Todd and Ma Baxter could handle the nation's economy, security and spiritual health all by their little selves, or so my Dad snarled sarcastically at the radio. As for the TV, I was amazed the screen was still intact.

'Cassaaahn-dra,' drawled Griff now. 'Two words. Publicity Stunt.'

'Meaning what?'

'Well, apart from being rhyming slang for Bishop Todd, *obviously* it means the man would do anything for two column inches in the *Messenger*.'

'It'll be more than two column inches,' I said. 'They reckon he's been kidnapped.'

Griff shrugged, lit another cigarette, and blew the smoke out the window.

I thought Griff might have shown a little more interest. Griff, after all, used to dote on Bishop Todd Lamont, though that was back when only Griff's hair was pale and he used to smile more, and eat a lot more, and Bishop Todd was merely Rector Todd. *Just call me Todd!* Griffin had idolised him – Todd being funny and magnetic and ambitious, a smiling bundle of charisma – and my brother's hero-worship drove my father to distraction, since he loathed the man. Todd's handsomeness was turning into that slightly fat self-importance that's exacerbated by a cassock, but I never really understood Dad's visceral loathing.

When Todd was elected Bishop, I walked in on my father and found him banging his head on his desk. I mean, literally banging it. Dad did not notice me – too busy trying to give himself brain damage – so I backed out and sucked on a knuckle. The banging stopped, after a bit, and I eased the door open. He still didn't notice me.

This was the only time I've seen my father cry. He had his hands in his hair and he was staring at his little wooden crucifix (suspect and idolatrous, but he shoved it in the desk drawer whenever the doorbell rang) and going *Why? Why? Why would you let him?* over and over again.

I decided that whatever I had to ask wasn't so important after all, because I didn't want to know what was wrong. It didn't look like the kind of thing I could help with, the kind of thing anyone could, so there was no point letting him know I was there.

I suspected it was the Griff Thing. I knew there had been a terrible falling-out. I knew Griff had done something wrong, and it must have been terribly wrong, because Griff wasn't allowed to serve at the altar any more when Arch-Rector Todd – as he was by then – came to officiate at Dad's church. But I didn't know why. I was young and my recollections of that time were hazy. I knew only that there were arguments and rows and a lot of anger, but falling out with Todd wasn't an option. He and Dad were One Church clerics, and the One Church was about unity more than anything else. It was terrified of a return to the days of quarrelling sects, of religious wars, of marginalised and dying faiths. That was why disunity was stamped on from a terrific height. If I understood very little else, I could at least understand that.

Well, after Todd was elected Bishop, my father had to get on with it, Todd being his boss and spiritual superior and all. There was much gnashing of paternal teeth, but no more tears. I never saw my father cry again.

Griff interrupted my thoughts. 'Who could be bothered kidnapping Fat Todd?'

'Anglican terrorists, they think.' I shrugged. 'Or Aiken-heads, or extremist schismatics. Might even be atheists. Poor old Todd.'

'Uh-huh.' Griff, unsympathetic, prodded at his console. 'Water still rising, is it?'

For a moment I couldn't think what he was talking about, and then I remembered that of course the low-lying streets of town were three feet deep in brown sludge, as they quite often were. Which was one of the nice things about living on the posh outskirts and halfway up a hill.

The floods – a once-in-a-century meteorological event (according to the Council) – had now happened three times in the last five years. The Council insisted they were going to do something about it. Perhaps they would have done, had the rain not fallen for seven straight days (again), the tide turned at the wrong time of day (again), the river mouth been half-silted up (again), and the surrounding farmland so short of topsoil that the water ran straight off it (as it always had done).

Griff and I were quite used to getting our wellies on and going to stare down at the river as it burst its banks in the gorge below the house, filled the valley with brown scummy water, and bulged into a torrent heading for the sea and the downstream, downmarket streets. One of our teachers had once tried to cross the valley by the back road during a flood and had been washed away in her car where the river gushed across the road. Fortunately for her she'd come to rest fifty yards downstream on a sandbank and some rubberneckers had made themselves useful and got her out, but it was a close-run thing and the rubberneckers themselves nearly went the way of all flesh when the car was ripped clear of the sandbank.

It had a split personality, our river. Beautiful, tame, rippling on a summer day, and a killer when it felt like it. Down among the alders in a sharp bend of the river, the river had dug out a cave as it swirled and turned, and it was one of our favourite hideouts, but you wouldn't believe the things we've found washed in there after a flood. Dr Shaw was nearly one of them.

Now I said to Griff, 'What if Todd went to look at the river and got washed away? He faffs around in the forest park. Rambling, pressing the flesh. You know what the riverbank's like.'

'Crumbly,' said Griff. 'Sandy. Wouldn't be surprised. So I wouldn't.'

'It's making the search a bit difficult too,' I said. 'Dogs can't get a scent. Ground's treacherous. They don't want to go too near the river themselves, a spokesman said so.'

'You know why they're not getting a scent,' said Griff. 'Todd's on an impetuous retreat to pray for the poor and dispossessed, and will be reappearing before press time on Monday.'

'Cynic,' I said.

'Yes, Bishop Todd has gone to follow his conscience, and since it has no idea where it's going either, they're both hopelessly lost.' He sucked on his Marlboro Light. 'Till Monday.'

'I thought you liked Bishop Todd,' I said.

'I did like Bishop Todd,' said Griff, 'and then I grew up.'

'You could have fooled me,' I said.

'Out. Out, out, out.' Griff rubbed his forehead with the heel of his hand, and singed his hair with the end of his fag. I could smell it.

'You've just...'

'OUT.'

• • •

My Dad was struggling to be sorry about Bishop Todd. He had a moral duty to be sorry, given what he does for a living, but I knew he wasn't sorry and he'd be happiest if Bishop Todd never came back at all. His black hair had fallen into his blue, blue eyes and for once he was not pushing it irritably away, because he thought it might hide what he was thinking. I could still read his eyes, though. I always could, up to a point. And he wasn't sorry.

See, here's the thing about Bishop Todd. While he's in the room – or the pulpit or whatever – you believe every word he says, to the point where you'd be slitting your wrists to get to Heaven faster. But as soon as he leaves, you just blink at yourself in the nearest mirror (unless you're my brother and you don't throw a reflection) and you think: What made me fall for that? It's like coming out of a shop with a pair of shoes you don't even like, and when you look in your bag you've bought the spray-on cleaner and the shoe trees too. And you're just way too ashamed of yourself to go back and ask for a refund.

And here's the thing with my Dad. He just stands up there looking not entirely sure of himself, and muttering the prayers a little darkly, and scratching his head and smiling sheepishly while he tries to make head or tail out of his Saturday-night handwriting. Then he gives everybody that devil-may-care grin, and shoves his hair out of his eyes, and races through the blessing. And you think: Who knows, there might just be something to all this.

So Dad was popular with the Faithful. He was a gentle type, good at comfort and consolation. Dad won a lot of souls for the One Church, in the early days (or at least talked them into not making a fuss). Maybe that's why he'd lasted so long, because he certainly wasn't so hot at the fire and brimstone bit and he'd never got very far up the career ladder. He was a troublemaker, consorting with jakies and whores and addicts, and he was always down the prison talking to the inmates, even seditious atheists. All of which made him a bit suspect, and Mum was forever covering up for him, which mostly involved being nice to thoroughly horrible high-ranking clergy. Like me, Mum was small and pathetically fragile, snappable as a dry twig, but deep down she was stronger than Dad. So I thought.

'For goodness' sake, Gabriel,' she said now, quietly, carving up a lasagne as if she was carrying out a post-mortem on someone she loathed, 'you've got Evening Worship at seven and you'd better pray for Todd's safe return.'

Yes, my Dad was called Gabriel. With a name like that he had to be either a priest or a gangster. Mind you, he looked more like a fallen angel: too handsome, in a worn-out sort of way, and his eyes fairly danced when he was in a cynical mischievous mood.

'I don't think I can do insincere prayer,' he mumbled now.

Mum's eyes flashed and I thought for a minute she'd snap at him. But she only said, very intensely, 'You can and you have.'

Dad glanced up at her and their eyes met again, that telepathic way they did at my grandmother's funeral, but this time I couldn't imagine what they were telling each other. I gave Griff a look but he was doing food-art with his lasagne and wouldn't look back at me.

'Yeah, Dad,' he said. 'Who's going to know? It's not like there's anyone listening.'

Practically choking on my lasagne, I put my hand over my mouth. I was really shocked. It was what I thought too, secretly, but *secretly* was the operative word; I'd never say it in front of the parents. Apart from anything else I was scared it would hurt Dad's feelings. With my brother I thought Dad would blow a fuse, but all he did was look at Griff rather sadly, saying nothing.

Mum did, though. Her knife and fork clattered onto her plate. 'Don't you dare blaspheme like that,' she hissed. 'Not in this house and *certainly not outside it.*'

Even Griff hesitated nervously. My heart was fairly banging against my ribs.

Griff recovered fast. 'Cool it, Mum. They stopped burning heretics, you know.'

'The way it's going,' said Dad, not quite *sotto voce* enough, 'they'll be starting again.'

Mum shot him a killer glare, but she had her composure back. 'You listen to me, Griffin. You have a nice enough lifestyle, and you may not appreciate it now but you would if you lost it. So don't you go endangering your father's career,' she glanced at Dad, 'any more than he does himself.' There was affection in her voice, though, and Dad lifted his downcast eyes to give her one of his loveliest smiles.

Mum wasn't finished with Griff. 'As for your own career, you're seventeen years old, you'll be leaving school soon. Get real, Griffin. Start thinking about it.'

'Thinking for myself, you mean?' Griff held up a bit of pasta on his fork and examined it.

'I take it you won't be training for the clergy,' snapped Mum, 'but you'll have to show a little more devotion if you want to get anywhere in life. You'll have to get your faith back,' and she added in a mutter, 'or at least pretend.'

'I haven't lost my faith, Mum,' said Griff, actually swallowing a shred of pasta. He gave her a beatific smile. 'I lost my religion.'

Mum looked at Dad but Dad only looked at his plate. I felt as if someone had hit me in the back of the head with a sock full of mud. I couldn't believe my brother would say such things in front of Dad, and Dad would just sit there and smile secretively at his lasagne.

Besides, I may think it's all mumbo-jumbo but deep down, I'm hedging my bets. It'd be a nasty shock to get to the end of that tunnel of light, only to meet the glowering bearded face of my Sunday School nightmares, arms folded and fingers drumming on the desk. And suddenly remember that not only did the demon dog eat my homework, I've carved something blasphemous on my desk and he's read it.

Guilt. It's my upbringing.

'Anyway,' Griff was saying, 'I know what I'm going to do. I'm going to be a teacher.'

'Are you trying to provoke me?' said Mum wearily.

'Mo-*therrr*,' said Griff. 'Teaching is a proud and respected profession.'

'Unless you plan to do something provocative and get yourself killed.'

Griff dropped his fork to his plate. I knew he'd really lost his temper because his face was stark white and his ears burned red. 'The militias killed that woman in cold blood. She didn't *get herself killed*, they killed her. And everybody acts like it was her fault!'

'The killer's been jailed, Griff,' said Dad.

'Three years! He'll be out in eighteen months. He's the criminal. What she did wasn't illegal!

'She offended a lot of people, Griffin,' sighed Mum. 'What did she expect?'

'She told her class Creationism wasn't proper science. That's not a crime!'

'Yet,' muttered Dad.

Mum rumpled his hair and Griff's simultaneously. 'That militia boy was a devout member of the One Church. There's a lot of them about, and don't you forget it, boys.'

Dad slapped her rear end, then winked at me as she whacked the top of his head, but Griff wasn't about to be bought off. 'Murder's still a crime, as far as I know, and whoever bombed that doctor's surgery hasn't even been caught. Know why? Because they're *not looking*.'

'Abortion's a crime,' I pointed out. Griff gave me a look of contempt.

'Yeah, but they didn't waste time with a courtroom, did they? And were the five people in the waiting room aborting anybody?'

'Conversation closed,' said Mum.

'Here's a new one, then. Why haven't you joined the Schismatic Movement, Dad?'

Dad's sigh had a tone of overstretched patience. 'I like my work, Griffin, and I do it quite well, and believe it or not there are people who need me, including a few in prison who'd agree with everything you say. And I'd rather not lose my job and the wage that goes with it. Okay?'

Even I thought that was a funny remark from a Man of the One God, with a vocation and everything. Mum gave him an incredibly dark look and drew her finger across her lips in a zipping motion.

'Griffin,' said Dad, 'what do you want? Sectarian wars? That's how it used to be.'

'Oh, okay. It sure is better now.'

Dad rubbed his temples. 'Religious wars are terrible things, Griff.'

'Yeah, slaughtering infidels is much more morally satisfying.' Griff's sneer didn't suit him. 'One Church! All power and no principles! The strains aren't sustainable.'

'Jeez, Griff,' I said witheringly, 'Did you get that line off a website?'

He slanted his eyes at me, just briefly enough to express his contempt. Then he pretended I hadn't said a word. 'The Church needs to split up. People should follow their own beliefs or none. And not get the crap beaten out of them for it.'

Dad shot me a wink. He'd seen the look Griff gave me, and he felt bad about it, and he wanted to make me feel better. I flashed a grin right back, and for a moment we were the only two people in the world, just having a laugh. Because you had to, sometimes, or you'd cry.

Left out, Griff reddened with rage and jealousy. There was a touch of desperation in his voice when he snapped, 'You believe in schism, Dad, I know you do!'

Dad gave him a warm smile. I think it was meant to reassure Griff, to include him, but the way things were round that table, it seemed a tiny bit patronising. 'Yes, Griff, I do. Which doesn't mean I have to broadcast the fact.'

'I find you contemptible,' said Griff. He cut his eyes away from Dad to glower at Mum. 'Both of you.'

I studied the tablemat and hoped this was going to be over soon. At least he hadn't included me in that assessment, which I'd have expected him to do, but he was giving me a glare anyway: I could feel it on the top of my scalp.

'You're seventeen years old, Griffin,' said Mum mildly. 'Of course you find us contemptible.'

'And one day you'll be twenty-seven,' added Dad, 'and then thirty-seven, and you'll be behaving contemptibly too. And know what? You'll be justifying it beautifully to yourself.'

There was a truly horrible silence that I couldn't interpret. I had an overwhelming urge to slide under the table and clasp my hands over my ears till they'd all gone away.

'Your *wage*!' Griff pushed his plate away. 'I'd rather live in a hovel than live in fear!'

'No you wouldn't, dear,' Mum told him placidly. 'You wouldn't have *Hell Breaker II* or nearly enough cigarettes.'

Dad snorted. Griff had no snappy comeback, so despite his vermilion ears, the conversation really was closed.

2: Cancellations

I was supposed to meet Ming that Saturday but I'd barely shouted goodbye to the parents and slammed out of the door when I came to a guilty halt. Chewing my nails, I pulled out my mobile. My Macbeth essay was already overdue and Dr deVilliers had made it plain yesterday morning that I was for extra detention if it wasn't on her desk first thing Monday. Which would be worse? Detention, or not seeing Ming?

My thumb hovered over his speed dial number as I pulled the gate closed. I hadn't seen him since he got suspended for blasphemy (again). On the other hand, did I want to get suspended myself? It occurred to me what my mother would have to say to that, so I came to a halt. Sighing, I tensed my thumb on Ming's number.

Then my phone wailed the *Rector Who* theme, and I jumped.

I put my hand to my heart. A reprieve. Might even be Ming himself. I punched a button and said, 'Hello?'

I frowned. Nothing but mumbled words and a distant clatter. A faint voice rose over some kind of interference. *'Gabriel, what happened to you on Thursday?'*

Oh, for crying out loud. I raised my eyes skywards. Dad did this all the time and he'd never learn. He never locked his keypad and he kept his ancient phone stuck in his back pocket and then he'd lean his backside on something and it would call back the last number. One of these days he'd be slagging off Ma Baxter or something and his phone would call the Archbishop or the prison governor and then he'd really be in trouble.

'Dad,' I said. 'Oy, *Dad*.' I didn't want to shout into my phone because there were people walking past and I'd look a bit stupid.

'What d'you mean, what happened to me?' crackled Dad's cross voice.

'Hey! *Dad!*' I said more loudly.

The crash of a saucepan onto the drainer drowned me out, so I took the phone away from my ear, wincing. Sitting down on the low wall of our neighbour's house, I waited for the racket to stop so I could catch Dad's attention. He was making a fearsome amount of noise clattering the pans around, and there was a gurgling rumble of interference that I reckoned was the dishwasher. I could have hung up but I couldn't resist giving him a hard time about this again. Dad and his mobile had never really got along.

Besides, it was quite sweet listening in on the parents. I liked hearing them banter and take the mickey out of each other, even when they were quarrelling. It was the sound of family, the sound of security.

'What I mean,' came Mum's distant voice, 'is what happened to your meeting with the Wardens?'

Dad paused an awfully long time for such an innocuous question. 'I hadn't got those figures they wanted,' he said at last. 'No point without them, so I called it off.'

'But you rang the accountants on Tuesday. I thought you said you...'

'No. Yes. I called but they couldn't give me the numbers. Okay?' His voice was uncharacteristically sharp.

Mum paused. 'I see. Okay.'

Silence fell, so I could have jumped in and caught Dad's attention, but instinct made me press the phone close to my ear and suppress my breathing. The Wardens ran the church and the Wardens ran Dad. Some of them were all right: I liked Brother Jonathan, and Brother Darren, and Sister (Amazing) Grace. But three of them I didn't like. They had hard little eyes that saw everything, right down to your soul, and they never stopped watching. Wardens were there, said Dad, because they were cheaper for the One Church than CCTV. Dad wouldn't cancel a meeting with the Wardens, not unless he had a very good reason.

Besides, Mum and Dad's conversation was not the cosy back-and-forth banter of security, it was alien and scary and punctuated by dead moments. Now Mum took an audible breath. 'If you'd let me know, we could have gone for a walk together.'

'You'd already left when I got back. I came out looking for you but I didn't know where to start.' Silence. 'Where *did* you go?'

Silence. 'Up to the fields beyond the steading. You didn't see me at all?'

'No, Brenna. No, I didn't. I, ah… I didn't go that way.'

I did not like the way this conversation was going. I *so* did not.

Mum's voice trembled. 'Gabriel, I want to talk to you about Griff and we never seem to get a chance.'

'I know.'

Silence, silence. I hated these vacuums of sound.

'You've been avoiding me, Gabriel. You don't want to have this conversation.'

'No, Brenna, I don't.' Dad slammed a pan down hard onto the steel drainer, making my phone buzz. 'I'm sorry.' He took an audible breath. 'I'll try.'

Mum said, 'Griff's never got over it, you know.'

With my phone pressed hard to my ear, I swung one leg over the low wall and then, more awkwardly, the other. Glancing up at the neighbours' windows, I could see no movement, no lights, and their car wasn't in its drive. Wouldn't be the first time I'd taken a shortcut through their garden, anyway, since Griff and I were always forgetting our front door keys. The phone at my ear crackled with tension, and holding my breath I pressed myself through the overgrown laurel arch and down the slabbed path past the plank fence that bordered our garden. Where the fence ended, an overgrown laburnum drooped across the slabs. Ducking beneath its poisonous yellow fronds, I peered down our own garden and through the kitchen window, just ten metres away. This was serious eavesdropping, I thought. I shouldn't do this. I should hang up now.

'I'm worried for Griffin, I really am. You need to talk to him, Gabriel.'

I could see them through the kitchen window. Their eyes weren't connecting like they always did; they were actively avoiding one another's gaze and touch. It was like looking at impostors. Alien bodysnatchers.

'Brenna,' said Dad. 'I've tried to talk to him. He's practically a man. He's dealt with it in his own way. I can't *make* him open up to me.'

'He wasn't a man when it happened.' Mum's voice had a break in it but her pitch had risen. I could hear her fine. 'I don't care how old he is. He's not over it.'

'You know why he's not over it,' said Dad. 'Because of us. We let a sick little abuser get off scot-free. We let Griff down. Of course he despises us, we're cowards. Especially me.'

'You're a *realist*,' she snapped.

'Oh, hardly,' said Dad. There was terrible bitter cynicism in his voice. I couldn't see his eyes properly but I knew they wouldn't be dancing. My stomach tightened and flipped.

'More than you let on,' said Mum.

'And that's one *you're* never to repeat in public.'

Mum was drying the lasagne dish over and over again, turning it and turning it. 'He'd have got away with it anyway. He'd have got away with it and we'd have been vilified, our whole family dragged through the mud, and you out of a job at the end of it. Me too, probably. We'd be in the gutter. You know how long Todd's reach is!'

My head was so light I was afraid I was going to fall face-first into the nettles under the laburnum. I nearly did when Dad said, 'Where's Cass? Keep your voice down.'

'It's okay, she went out.'

'Does she know? Do you think she knows?'

'No. Let's keep it that way.' Mum massaged her temples with her thumb and forefinger.

Dad rubbed his soapy fist hard across his forehead. It was a gesture echoing hers, and that was reassuring in a small way, as if they couldn't help being reflections of each other, as if that was one thing that couldn't change.

'I hate this. I hate all these damn secrets. What's best for your children is not to know, never to know, never to be told. How is that right?'

'It's not right. It's *necessary*. What your children don't know about you, they can't let slip.' Mum said in a low voice, so I could only just make it out, 'You told me what he said.'

'Oh, sure.' Dad's voice was unbelievably bitter. '*I'm a much-loved holy man, Gabriel. Who knows you, besides whores and drunks and atheists? Mother Baxter is my friend, she depends on me. She'll never let anything happen to me. Who'll protect you, Gabriel?* Word for word, Brenna. I remember it word for word. You don't have to shove it down my throat.'

'That's why I should never have to remind you! Okay? We'll paper over the cracks, Gabriel. We've done it for four years, we can go on doing it. I know it's not ideal…'

'It's a bloody sin, Brenna!'

'It's the best we can do for our family. All right?'

'Yeah.' Dad drew his soapy hand down his face. 'Yeah, I know.'

Mum flicked a bit of lather off his nose. 'I know you know. You're a good man, Gabriel. You're doing your best.'

'I'm not, Brenna.' He gave a laugh that was awfully like a sob. 'I wish I was more like your sister. She's got a bit of spirit.'

'Spirit? Abby's lucky she doesn't get stoned in the street, the way she goes on.'

They exchanged a fond look and a dry awkward giggle, and I thought it was over. My thumb was hovering over the disconnect button, my pulse beating so hard in my throat it was almost choking me, when Dad spoke again.

'What if,' he said, and paused to swallow. 'What if Todd isn't coming back?'

'What?'

Dad draped a wet cloth over the tap, gripping the ends of it and leaning on it like it was holding him up. 'Maybe Todd isn't coming back, Brenna. Maybe he's in the river.'

'Don't get your hopes up.'

If it was a joke, neither of them laughed. Mum had stopped drying; she just stood there twisting the towel in her fingers. The gardens were on a slope and I was looking down over a raised drystone-walled bed into the kitchen, so I could see that the draining rack was empty.

'Gabriel?' Mum's voice was shaky and low. 'Do you know something about this?'

'What's that supposed to mean?' But Dad had turned and was looking into her eyes.

'I...' Mum averted her gaze from his cool steady one. 'Nothing. I worry, that's all.'

'Well, don't worry,' said Dad. 'Don't waste so much of your life worrying. I'll even stand up there tonight and pray for Todd. Okay? I might even mean it. Because maybe he is in that river, Brenna. And if he is, there really is a God.'

Dad's voice was expressionless. But his hands were back in the bowl and he was scrubbing at them, lathering the backs of them and rubbing Fairy Liquid under his fingernails. He kept doing it as I backed out of the laburnum branches, and ducked behind the fence, my heart slamming so hard against my ribs I was afraid they'd hear it.

It was pure bad luck that I had Macbeth in my fanciful head, because that was what it made me think of straight away, Lady Macbeth going *Out Damned Spot!* And if I hadn't, if I hadn't been so prone to wild speculation, I might not have done what I did.

You see, Dad says I have an overactive imagination. Dad says my mind takes me off on irrational tangents and leads me to deductions with no basis in reality. My father says a lot of things about me that I think are pretty rich coming from him, since I'm not the one who believes in a guy in the sky marking us all for Merit, Effort and General Comprehension.

I'm telling you this so you'll understand why I moved the Bishop's body.

3: Fugue

Cass doesn't know. Cass doesn't know.

But I ought to know. Perhaps I did know. If something so terrible had happened to Griff, I couldn't *not* know. Trouble was, I had a notion that none of this was a big surprise, that somewhere in my head I'd always known this dreadful thing.

But if it was in my head, it must be lost. Things got lost in my head very easily.

This was something to do with the fractured skull, I suppose, and I can tell you it's a very good reason for looking where you're going and not playing the fool around fast-moving traffic. My brain was absolutely fine most of the time, but at other times my inner chaos would catch up with me, and I'd have to stand very still and blank out the world for a bit. When my head was confused, I had to wait quietly till things came together and I understood where and who I was. It drove my teachers mad, but they could hardly tell me off, and it never lasted too long. If I blanked everything, the clamour in my head would eventually settle and subside. I could tuck it up beneath the covers, soothe it to sleep and forget about it, and I'd be just fine again, till the next time. Till the images and voices built to an incomprehensible jumble once more, and I'd have to calm them down all over again.

Voices in your head: that's not good. It's never good. I knew this, and I knew I had to keep them quiet. And if I couldn't keep them quiet, I must at least keep quiet about them.

So maybe that's where Griff's tragedy was, lost in that niggling cacophony, but I was too tired and afraid to filter it out and listen properly.

4: Flotsam

The first corpse I met that day was the rabbit. It was a real Disney character, its eyes almost bigger than its head, but the back half wasn't so cute, splayed flat and useless by the roadside a mile out of town. I suppose a car broke its spine.

I was on my way to meet Ming. I recoiled from the idea of standing him up, and besides, I'd lost the taste for Macbeth altogether. To hell with Cruella, I decided: I'll take the detention.

As I walked past the rabbit, I noticed its eyes weren't dead yet, but I tried to pretend they were, because I didn't want to deal with this. It was looking at me warily, as if to say it was fine, thanks very much, and perfectly happy with the situation. It might have got away with it if its velvet ear hadn't twitched.

Rocks are like policemen: only around when you don't need one. It took me forever to find a big enough stick, which was rough on the rabbit, because it knew perfectly well what I was up to. I hesitated, because it was adorable, but half-shut my eyes and hit it twice on the neck, then once more for luck. I opened my eyes, feeling a complete heel, and saw its hind leg jerk skywards, then sink gracefully back to the ground. When I poked it with the stick its head lolled loose on its fragile neck. There was blood trickling from its ear that was a simply beautiful colour: jewel-red, sparkling so vividly against the tarmac you'd think the rabbit's life had drained out of its eyes onto the road. I touched its unblinking eyeball with the tip of a finger, then snatched it away; it was dead now, all right. I shivered, and found myself walking faster after that, taking the forest track that led deep into the damp spidery pinewood.

I was still a bit shaken when I found Ming, who was sitting on a log reading a primer on Macbeth. He didn't look up, but thrust the book at me with a sigh.

'Cass, I don't know why I bother,' he said. 'I won't be back in time for the exams. Anyway, this guy talks rubbish.'

Typical Ming. Always thought he knew better than the experts, which was probably one reason he'd been suspended from school. The irritating thing was, he usually did know better. He read a lot, did Ming, probably because he was suspended so often. It wasn't entirely his fault: it was just that he was always sticking up for his mad secularist parents and getting into fights with the alpha-male thugs in the Scripture Corps (who never got suspended).

My hip ached from the long walk, so I sat down on the log beside him. This was our favourite log, deep in the ghost wood. The alleged haunting was only part of the reason nobody ever came here – well, nobody but me and Griff and Ming. The wood was overgrown and gloomy, the ground steep and treacherous, and we loved it. There was privacy here, secrecy even, and that was more precious than ever these days. And while my mother wasn't our biggest worry, it helped that she was unlikely to spot us here. Mum didn't disapprove of Ming, exactly, but she was a little bit Jane Austen about unsuitable matches that might spoil my life chances.

She needn't have worried. Ming had great bone structure behind his spots and his overlong dark blond hair, and one day he was going to be stunning, but not yet. That didn't stop him believing he was God's gift to me.

'So, hi gorgeous,' he said, with a killer smile.

I gave him what I hoped was a withering look. 'I'll get back to you when I'm desperate.'

'Did you hear about the Mad Mullah?'

'*Ming*,' I said, and then I laughed. 'Yeah. Griff reckons it's a publicity stunt.'

'Yeah?' Ming looked at me quite intently, his greenish eyes shiveringly bright.

'Uh-huh. Me, I think he's in the river.'

'I think you're probably right.' He stood up and dusted off the seat of his jeans. He had a new cut below his left eye, scabbed over but nasty-looking, and scratches on his cheek. The bruise from his jaw to his temple was ugly and swollen.

'You've been fighting again,' I said.

'Jeremiah Maclaren, the big pussy. He's sorry now. And they can't suspend me twice.'

I frowned. 'Are you okay?'

'More okay than him,' said Ming smugly.

I watched him watching me. There were times I was really afraid for Ming. It wasn't as if he was starting from pole position in life, being an infidel and everything. He'd tried to be very politically correct when his parents' land was confiscated and given to crofters of the Faithful, he'd been quite supportive, but that changed when the poor stunned crofters were declared economic failures, their government loan called in, and the land handed over to Ma Baxter's stepbrother's second cousin.

None of that ancient history ought to make him look quite so depressed right this minute. I hated to see him sad, so I gave him my best smile.

'So, *gorgeous*,' I said. 'Want to go look at the river?'

• • •

Arachnophobia is a misnomer. There is nothing irrational about a fear of spiders, any more than a fear of snakes or scorpions. Some spiders can kill you. So there.

Not these ones, admittedly, but it was always Ming's job to walk in front. That way, if he walked between two boo-by-trapped trees, he hit the webs first, and the surprised spiders ended up on his face and not mine. They were a pretty yellow and brown and they just hung there, and I didn't mind them as much as the leggy black household brutes, but I didn't want them on my face. Fortunately Ming had never minded being my fall guy.

In the space between two pines, he brushed his palm across his face and flicked his fingers. 'So how's that brother of yours?'

I dodged the spider's trajectory, and took a second to think. 'Fine.'

I doubted that now, but anyway, how would I know how my brother was? I didn't get much more from Griff these days than the odd contemptuous stare. Till now I'd reckoned it was one of those growing-up-and-apart things, that his old self must be in there still, like some secret identity. That one day he'd get over being Dark Griff and go back to just being Griffin.

'You'd know better than me,' I added. 'You see more of him than I do.'

'He wants to watch himself,' said Ming. 'The Scripture Corps have got it in for him.'

'Look who's talking. You just watch yourself too.'

Ming was scrambling down a flat mossy rock, but though it was a tricky manoeuvre he turned and gave me a dazzling smile. It made my insides clench, which did nothing but make me irrationally cross. Distracted, I slipped and banged my hip hard on the boulder. Ming grabbed first one hand and then the other, and held me until I finished sliding down on my rear end.

I stood up and shook him off. My hip hurt like billy-oh, being the one that took most of the impact of the car, so I rubbed it hard with the palm of my hand while I tried not to cry. I'm not the crying type but really, it hurt that much. So there I was, sore and humiliated, and I was getting angrier with Ming by the second. I hated that look he was giving me as he bit his lip, concerned and affectionate and a little penitent too.

'Are you okay? Sorry, Cass, that was my fault.'

'Don't be so flaming vain,' I snapped. 'How would it be your fault?'

He put up his hands, palms outwards, and took a step back. 'Whoo!' He was grinning.

A blush stung my cheeks. I was always overreacting around Ming, then feeling stupid about it, but I didn't want to fall out with him. 'Okay.' I grinned back. 'Sorry.'

'So you won't slap me if I hold your hand, then?'

I gave him a look. 'Why would you want to?'

'Jeez.' He rolled his eyes and took my hand anyway. 'To stop you falling on your backside? There's a steep bit coming up.'

In fact I quite liked the feeling of my hand in his. It gave me a safer feeling as we slip-slid together down the muddy rabbit-path, Ming grabbing for branches when he nearly fell himself. I was strangely reluctant to let go of him and hold onto branches myself, which must have made it even more precarious for him, but he didn't let go either, not even when we were safely on the track. He just turned to me and smiled like he'd made it through a dreaded exam.

He lifted my hand and looked at it. 'Ever ask yourself why you're so touchy?'

I snatched it away. 'I'm not *touchy*. I just don't like being pawed.'

His anger flared. 'Who's *pawing* you?'

'I didn't say you were. Oh, sorry. *Sorry*.' I raised my eyes heavenwards. 'Who's touchy now? I didn't mean it, okay?'

'Yeah? Prove it.' He stepped *way* too close and put his palm against my face like he was holding it still, except his touch was tentative. And then he kissed me right on the mouth.

My hand was splayed against his chest like I was shoving him away, except that to my surprise I wasn't shoving. From limited experience I could say he was a good kisser; at least, he wasn't asking for a jab in the solar plexus like the only other boy who'd ever got to me past the Scripture Corps Morality Patrol (Motto: 'Save Yourself: Save Your Soul').

If I had a soul, it had pretty much had it at that point. No question of shoving yet, that was for sure. Instead I could feel my fingers curling round a fistful of Ming's shirt as if I was actually trying to reel him in a bit closer. Then he ran his hand down the small of my back onto my backside and pulled me gently against him.

I swear, I was so shocked I nearly bit his tongue off. I yelped and he pulled back straight away, but he wasn't in the least bit fazed. He kept hold of my hand and turned away to look coolly over the lip of the slope that fell away from the track. 'Look at that,' he said, with nothing but mild interest.

I was so confused I just looked. About twenty feet below us the green tangle of twig and branch and overgrown grass gave way to brown devastation, the ground sodden and destroyed. There were great piles of broken branches and litter piled where the river had dumped them, and fringes of grubby white scum caught on the high water mark. Further down, the sullen river swirled around the base of trees, but it was almost back within its banks.

'It's gone...' I swallowed. 'S'gone down a lot.'

'Yeah,' said Ming, still staring down at it.

'A *lot*,' I said again, for something to say. I could feel the imprint of his body from my scalp to my toes, and my skin was tingling.

'It wasn't meant to do that,' he said.

'No. It was going to get worse before tonight. Always wrong, aren't they?' I was starting to feel better now that Ming was distracted, now that there was something to talk about. 'Hey, what's that?'

He started, and tried to grab my hand back, but I was

already edging down the slope. There was something big and white jammed behind a log. I didn't like the slope, and I liked the river at the foot of it even less, but for some reason I felt high, as happy-go-lucky as some eight-year-old kid and just as curious. And immortal. And I wanted to prove I didn't need my hand held, that shattered hip or no shattered hip, I wasn't scared of steep muddy slopes like some fainting heroine in an Empire-line dress. And let's face it, I was showing off.

'Cassandra!' shouted Ming. God, just like my mother. *Cassandra!*

I turned back to take the mickey out of him, which was when the lance of pain shot up my right side. Must have been falling against the boulder that had done it, as if my hip had suddenly remembered it had been *hurt*, damn it. There was no arguing with that leg when it decided to go. I was furious with it even before my foot went from under me and I began to slide. Struggling to get my balance, I took a couple of hops, then two lopsided running steps, my right leg still refusing to take any weight. Careering on down the slope, I caught both feet on a jutting birch branch and went flying, right over the log and the white thing.

It knocked the breath out of me, but that was just fright, because I'd mostly landed on something soft, my ankles hooked over the log, my shoulders and face in the scummy mud. I lay there feeling scared and not wanting to look at what I was lying on. I'd had a fleeting glimpse as I sailed over it and must have registered what it was, but just for the moment I wasn't letting that visual image connect with my brain.

What did I see? I don't dream about it but I still see it sometimes in that funny shadowland between being awake and being asleep: that moment when your body jolts and you realise the slideshow in your head wasn't real. That's when I'll see again what I saw then, and think that it's lying beside me in the bed. A bloated thing in a cassock. A lolling head that isn't quite the right shape. Curled puffy fingers that aren't quite the right colour. And sticking out of the cassock, one foot, booted, on the end of a leg that isn't at quite the right angle.

Ming was crashing down the slope behind me. I could hear his panting breath as he skidded to a halt so that he didn't end up in the same undignified position as me. Very clearly and quietly, I heard him blaspheme.

'Jesus Christ.'

Clambering down around the log, he grabbed my arms to haul me to my feet. I had to clutch his shirt and then his shoulders to get myself upright and steady, but neither of us was worrying about Young Lust at that moment. Something lifted in my throat and I swallowed hard. With Ming gripping me tightly, we stood and stared.

'Somebody bashed the Bishop,' said Ming.

Well, I guess he had his composure back. I snorted and giggled, because I couldn't help it, and because I couldn't think what else to do.

What else was there to do, anyway? There was no question of trying to resuscitate the…*Thing*. It had a smell about it, and it wasn't the Odour of Sanctity. It occurred to me that the smell had got onto me and I would never get it off, not as long as I lived. I started to shake, and Ming's fingers tightened on my arms, but we still couldn't look away.

It wasn't like the rabbit. Bishop Todd was not cute now, if he ever had been, and I'll tell you, I wasn't about to touch his eyeball. Near his head lay a rough stone about the size of a big man's fist, and it was sticky with a dark congealed smear that was neither bright nor sparkling. Otherwise there didn't seem to be much blood. Perhaps it had washed away in the water that swirled around his foot, making it move slightly as if he was lying there cooling his hot toes. A corner of mud-stained cassock drifted in the tiny sidelined current.

Ming wasn't making a wild guess about the cause of death. There was a great shattered hollow in the side of the head, but I must have been in denial.

'He fell in the river,' I said, and I was amazed how steady my voice was. 'See, I was right. He fell in the river up at the forest park, and he washed downstream. Must've hit his head on the way. See?'

'No,' said Ming, crouching to prod the horrible wound with a twig. He wanted to be a doctor, did Ming. Fat chance, but I suppose he felt he should be able to do something like that. He recoiled as the twig went in too far, as if he was scared he'd hurt the broken head, but then he jabbed it gently again, as if he couldn't help himself. His hands had just been touching me, I thought, and now they were touching the Bish – the *Thing*.

'He's maybe been eddying around here when the water was high,' he said. 'But he's not been in the river. His cassock's wet but he's still wearing it.'

'So?' I don't know why I felt so defensive. My thoughts hadn't sorted themselves out yet.

'It'd come off in the river. I read that once in a – '

'You read too much,' I told him with a shudder. 'I still think…'

'Nah.' He nodded at the lump of bloody stone. 'That's what hit him. That wouldn't wash downstream with him, would it?'

Well. All right.

It wasn't unusual that Bishop Todd – what was left of him – was wearing his cassock. It was an affectation of his. Famous for it, and he liked to be recognised, did Bishop Todd. Bet he was regretting it now, wherever he was. If somebody came after you with a big rock it wouldn't be easy to run away in a cassock.

The Bishop's hands were pale and bloated, and his fingers reminded me of grubs you might turn up underneath a rock, a rock that hadn't been moved for a long time. Those hands seemed to me the most horrific thing about him. They were worse than his face, worse even than his head. The protruding leg was pale too, whiter than white and blotched blue and grey, scattered with spiky hairs, puffy at the ankles around the tightly-laced walking boot. It was ugly but it wasn't as horrible as his grub-hands.

'What are we going to do?' Ming stood up and stared down thoughtfully at the Thing.

I stared at *him*. 'What do you mean, what are we going to do?'

'I mean, I suppose we ought to call the police.'

And that was the first time it occurred to me that we didn't have to.

• • •

We stood in silence for a while. When I say silence, of course, I'm not counting the whooshing of wind high in the pines, and the rustle of beasts in the forest litter, and the subdued roar of the river, and the pounding of our own blood in our ears. I stared down at the broken grass and churned earth, trying not to look at the Bishop's head, making myself focus on his feet instead, his feet in their tight-laced walking boots.

And while we stood there, time at a complete halt around us, the switch happened. Ming turned into a bundle of shredded nerves: I could practically feel it happen to him. And I was suddenly in complete control of myself, calm and confident. Needs must.

'Listen,' said Ming abruptly. 'When you report this can you leave me out of it?'

'Why?' The question was irrelevant, but I asked it to pass the time, while the wheels of my disordered mind turned and spun and clicked into place. What was his problem? I knew for a fact that Ming had nothing to fear. For a *fact*. I, on the other hand...

'Only, Cass, it's not going to look good, me finding him... it...you know. With my parents and all?' The words began to tumble out of him. 'And getting suspended, and all the fights? And – and the *land*. Mum and Dad's estate. You know?'

'I don't see what that's got to do with anything.' Completely, totally, unbelievably irrelevant. I wished he'd shut up for a minute so I could think what to do.

'Cass.' There was panic in his voice. He seized my arm. 'Come over here, come away from...*that*.'

He pulled me into the shade of a huge pine, though I

kept looking back at the body. 'Listen, Ma Baxter's step-brother's second cousin? The one they gave our land to after the crofters failed?'

'In inverted commas. Yeah.' *Shut up, Ming, shut up, I need to think…*

He crouched and tugged me down beside him, as if someone might see us. 'It was only in his name, wasn't it? It was a holding company. It was Bishop Todd got the land.'

'Really?' I blinked at him. That did shock me. 'Really, Ming?'

'Yeah, really. Don't ask me how I know, it doesn't matter. It's just… it doesn't look good. That's all.'

I could see his point. It'd be different if Ming's parents had humbly accepted the change in their circumstances, which they might have done if their confiscated estate had stayed in the hands of the crofters, who I think they quite liked. But it turns out that militant atheists – which they were by then, if not before – weren't good at keeping their mouths shut and their opinions to themselves. Ming's parents were always in trouble, and quite often in the police cells for a night or two. My Mum and Dad, of course, couldn't afford to have anything to with seditious political activists, but to give them their due, neither set of parents tried to come between me and Ming. I think they hoped the authorities wouldn't bother with a friendship between kids. So I went on going over to stay at his poky new house in the bad part of town, squashed onto the floor in my sleeping bag in the sitting room. And Ming went on coming over to stay with us, where he got a whole spare room to himself, which I tried not to feel guilty about. Dad worried more about us now that we were getting older, because once we were of age it would be an Unauthorised Relationship with the potential for carnality (underage carnality was something the government didn't even acknowledge, officially). But Dad never complained, and Mum only very occasionally said something level-headed and astringent about How These Things Looked.

What it came down to was this: Ming being in the vicinity of a dead Bishop, and the one who stole his parents' land, did not have the angelic sheen of innocence.

'No,' I said. 'It's not going to look very good.'

'And finding the body, Cass. That's bad too. If you find the body you're a prime suspect. It's a well-known fact.'

I bit my nails hard. 'You *so* read too much.'

'It's not that I had anything to do with…I don't want you to think…I mean, I wouldn't…'

'Of course you wouldn't,' I said. 'Of course I don't think that.'

'Okay.' He breathed a huge sigh. 'So give me a head start, okay? Twenty minutes, say. Twenty minutes won't make any difference. Then you can report it.'

'We're not reporting it.'

Ming just stared at me. But I watched the brown gushing river and smiled.

I said, 'It's really gone down a lot, hasn't it?'

• • •

'You are *not* serious!' Ming's eyes were so wide the whites of them showed all around his irises.

'I'm totally serious.' I shrugged. 'We have to hide it. That's all.'

'What d'you mean, *hide* it?'

'*Duh*. We put it where nobody can find it.' I sighed patiently. 'You're the expert. They can't prove a murder if there isn't a body. Isn't that right?'

'Well, that's not quite... actually it depends on...Cass, why are we even discussing this?' I had never seen a face as white as Ming's was, right then. '*He's been murdered!* Why do we want them not to prove it?'

Because the river was supposed to rise. Because it had gone down instead. Because there wasn't enough force in the water now to wash the thing out to sea.

Because the killer must have panicked, conscience-stricken. He must have run, run like the hounds of Hell were after him, when he should have waited to roll the Bishop into the crashing mountainous water. Because he must have hoped afterwards that the river had risen anyway. The way it was supposed to...

If he's in the river, there really is a God...

But he wasn't. And I wasn't leaving him here, that was for sure, but nor could I shove him into the tamed river. Drifting, eddying, the furthest the Bishop would get was the low bridge under the bypass. I thought about him, stuck there in the brown water, that pale foot in the air like Excalibur, crowds gathering. It was not something I could contemplate.

I said, 'You're not going to believe me. But help me anyway. Help me hide it.'

'Cass, I can't touch that thing.' He was trembling.

I frowned. 'You just touched it. You just picked up that stick and...'

'Yes,' he snapped. 'Okay. But I don't want to touch it

again. I don't want to pick it up, I *don't want anything to do with it*. I don't want to take it anywhere.'

'It's not far.'

'That's not the *point!*' He grabbed my hand. 'Cass, what's your problem? What makes you want to…'

'See that?' I said calmly.

Bewildered, he looked at the ground where I was pointing. You could make out the print of a walking boot, at least half the sole and the whole of the heel, and between them, a very distinct design of an alligator. 'Uh-huh,' he said.

'And see that?' I pointed at the Bishop's boot.

He didn't say anything. He didn't have to. There wasn't an alligator on it, that was all.

'My Dad did this.' I snatched my hand out of Ming's and massaged it with my fingers, though he hadn't hurt it. 'Understand? Dad killed the Bishop.'

• • •

He didn't say *You're mad* or *You're crazy* or *Don't talk such mince*. He just shoved his hair out of his eyes with both hands, then clasped his hands behind his head.

'Why do you think he'd do that, Cass?'

Old Mister Analytical. Not *Why would he do that?* Just *Why do you think he would?*

'I really haven't got time for this.' I was amazed at how cool and determined I felt. The fact was, I had no choice, and we'd better get it done quickly. Ming had to be on my side, he absolutely had to, just like he always had been. 'Okay, here's how it is. Dad hates Todd.'

'So do a lot of people.'

'No, Ming. You do. Most people think he's great,' I said bitterly. 'Even if half the world hated him, it wasn't them out here walking on Thursday when he went missing. It was my Dad. And he wanted Todd dead. I heard him say so.'

'Lots of people have those Alligator boots,' he said weakly.

'No,' I said. 'They don't. They're imported. You can hardly get them for love or money and Mum had to go on a six-month waiting list before Dad's birthday.'

He could see there was no point following that tack, so he fell silent. His eyes narrowed and it made me shiver, because I'd actually assumed Ming would howl with laughter and throw my arguments straight out of court. Instead he was taking me seriously, and that unnerved me.

'What do you think his motive would be, Cass?'

There it was again. Not *Why would he have a motive?* It was, *What do you think his motive would be?*

'You're not going to believe it,' I said.

'Try me.' His eyes were very wary now.

The words tumbled out of me in a rush. 'Todd did something awful to Griffin. He abused him. Assaulted him. Oh God, I don't know.' *I didn't want to know, either. I never wanted to know.*

Ming's jaw had gone all loose. So loose he couldn't even speak.

'Four years ago. I've worked it out, Ming!'

He found his voice. 'Cass. Oh, my God. Cassandra. What makes you think that?'

What makes me think that!

'Stop asking me those stupid questions!' I yelled. 'I

heard them, okay? I heard Mum and Dad talking about it! I never knew because they never told me! They never told *anyone!* Todd threatened them, he threatened Dad with all sorts of things.'

'Stop, stop. How do you imagine he would…'

'Griff used to serve at the altar, remember? Todd was always coming to preach at our church. Dad was sick of him, he was always…' My eyes widened as something horrible struck me. 'Oh, Ming, maybe that's why. Maybe it was so he could hang around Griff. And Griff worshipped Todd!' I felt like crying but I was too angry. 'It must have been just before he was elected Bishop. Dad couldn't do a thing. His word and Griff's against this powerful guy who was going to be Bishop and everybody knew it! A friend of Ma Baxter's!'

Ming was shaking his head, really slowly, his fingers still gripping the back of it. 'Oh, my God,' he kept saying, over and over again. Funny coming from him. 'Oh my God.'

'You believe me,' I said. 'You know it's true.' I was torn between triumph and sheer horror, because I was right. The look on Ming's face told me so.

'Cass,' he said again, but no sound came out.

I looked at him. Then I looked again. 'You knew,' I breathed.

'No!' His panic was back and that proved it.

'You knew about this!'

'Cassandra, please believe me. I didn't. I did not know any such thing!'

I wanted to believe him, I really did.

'Cass,' he pleaded. 'Forget about this. What you're thinking of doing, it's crazy.'

'*Forget it?*' Glaring at him, I spoke clearly so he'd understand, ticking off my points on the fingers of one hand. 'Dad cancelled his meeting with the Wardens. Nobody *ever* does that. He came out walking, but Mum didn't see him because he was here in the wood. There's his footprint. He hated Todd, everybody knows it, and I don't blame him!'

'You're jumping to conclusions,' mumbled Ming through his hands. 'Crazy ones.'

'Look.' I tried to be patient with him. 'This is a lucky break. Maybe it's a sign, maybe we were meant to find him! I've never seen Todd in these woods before, have you?'

I'd never seen anyone but us. It was too wild, too steep, the ground was too treacherous. It was child-unfriendly and dog-unfriendly, dark and spidery and oppressive. There weren't forest walks and cycle tracks and play areas, like there were up at the forest park. Besides, it was meant to be haunted.

Certainly was now.

I sighed. 'There's nobody here for Todd to talk to. He can't posture and preach and show off to ghosts. That's why they haven't thought of searching here yet.'

'Cass, they think he's been abducted by rebels. That's why they're not looking here. They're not expecting to find his rotting corpse, they're waiting for the demands!'

'Ah.' I made a dismissive gesture. 'But why was he here at all?'

Ming eyed me. 'Go on.' Like he was humouring a madwoman.

'Well,' I said. 'Suppose Dad arranged to meet him. Maybe he wanted to talk to Todd, in the most private place he could think of, somewhere they wouldn't be disturbed. Maybe it just got out of hand. I'm sure it was an accident, Ming. I'm sure it was, but they mustn't find... this. They'll search here eventually, don't you see that? If it stays here it'll be found.' I hesitated. 'Him. Sorry, I mean *him.*'

'Your Dad couldn't do this,' said Ming mechanically. 'It was somebody else.'

'Like who?' I gritted my teeth in frustration. 'Look, the Whistling Gypsy Rover could have done it, it doesn't matter. Dad cancelled his meeting, he came out here, his DNA must be all over the place. My Dad will get the blame!'

Ming didn't speak. I didn't know what he was thinking and that was unusual.

'Listen,' I snarled. 'You don't want to be involved in finding this? Fine. Okay. You do this one thing for me and *neither of us* will be involved.'

He looked at me like he didn't even know me.

'Are you threatening me, Cass?' he asked quietly.

'No,' I said.

We both knew it was a lie.

• • •

The Thing was heavy, heavier than I expected. I never knew what the term *dead weight* meant till I had one of the Bishop's legs under each arm, his booted feet flopping loose and banging my thighs as I struggled awkwardly down the hill, trying to ignore the twinges of pain in my hip. I felt no fear, and not a shred of pity, which was funny when I'd had nothing against the man till a few hours ago. All I felt was revulsion.

Worse, my head was starting to echo, thoughts and images were beginning to clamour and if I didn't keep a firm grip on my brain, they'd get out of hand. Determinedly I shoved down the lid on the voices, shutting them up. Now was not a good time.

It would have been fairer, this being my bright idea, for me to take the head end. But Ming insisted. It was the heaviest bit, he said, and he was stronger, and we'd get this done faster if I'd just *shut up*. His arms were locked around the Bishop's chest, his fingers clasped together over his breastbone as if in prayer – ironic, since he'd never darkened a church door in his life – and the damaged head was jammed against Ming's ribs. Luckily there was no blood dripping or anything. Ming said there wouldn't be. Smart aleck. Bookworm.

Tripping on lichened branches, stumbling on roots and hollows, we almost fell several times. To get flat safe access to the river, we actually had to clamber uphill a bit, over a shoulder of ground and down again. Where the river widened, where it wasn't all churning rapids, there was a flat pebbly beach about two metres long, leading to a long stretch of calmer water by the bank. If we could get in there we could wade fifty metres downstream, floating the Bishop like a log. But we had to get there first.

I ought to be crying or panicking, but there was more of that in Ming's white face. All I wanted to do was laugh. I thought how ridiculous we must look, slathered in mud and grass and twigs, hauling a fat and slightly malodorous clergyman down to the river, sliding and stumbling and cursing. Ming cursed, anyway, over and over again. I said nothing. I needed all my breath for the slope, and besides,

I had this terrible fear of laughing.

We paused on the swirling edge of the flood, and Ming said, 'Be careful,' but I felt more immortal than ever as we waded gingerly into it. At knee-depth the tug of the current wasn't too strong but we wouldn't want to be going much deeper, that was for sure. Out in midstream the river still boiled and raced, heaping brown water against unseen rocks. Ming's fair hair was falling into his eyes and his chin was resting now on the Bishop's broken head, the body sagging in his arms. Through the strands of sweat-damp hair his eyes were very green and very scared, and he looked a lot more exhausted than I felt.

'There,' I gasped at last, and nodded. The bend of the river was ahead, together with the half-submerged secret cave where pirates and orcs and cowboys had once fought fierce cross-genre battles with plastic swords and cap guns. The memory made me hesitate for the first time, but then I thought: Well. It's not a game any more, is it?

'We're fine,' I said.

Ming just looked at me.

The cave mouth was well hidden and even at the best and driest of times you had to wade into the river to reach it. Now we floated our revolting burden in on the current, keeping hold of handfuls of cassock just to be on the safe side. We didn't want it drifting off into the main torrent and pulling away from us. Then came the hardest part, because we had to duck into the concealed entrance, tugging the Bishop awkwardly after us. The river swirled into the cavern like it must have done aeons back, when glacial ice carved it. That was a strange thought but comforting. It gave everything perspective. The river must have seen stranger things over the millennia, though it was hard to imagine what. Cowboys battling orcs, maybe.

Where the edge of the water lapped the cave floor we hauled the Thing onto dry land. The cave was cool and gloomy but it felt familiar, and it was much easier to drag the body, a leg each this time, across the smooth grainy sand. We took it as far as we could, bending double ourselves, till we found a ledge of rock that would take a body jammed underneath it.

'The sand's wet,' said Ming. His hoarse voice echoed too loudly and made me jump.

'Yeah,' I said. 'It must have filled right up when the flood was higher.'

Blood throbbed painfully in my temples, and I had that horrible choked feeling in my throat again, and a rising clamour in my head. *No.* Get a grip, I told myself. I stared hard into the dimness, seeing nothing clearly, concentrating on smothering the voices. I breathed in, I breathed out. I did it again. I pictured a pillow, pictured myself shoving it down over them. Gradually they fell silent, and I could let myself look at the real world again.

There was enough light for me to see Ming scrabbling at the sand with his fingers, digging out a hollow and frantically trying to shove the Bishop tighter under the shelf of rock.

'It's okay,' I said. I sounded very calm. 'The water's going down.'

'This is crazy,' said Ming again, breathless. 'They'll find him.'

'No they won't.' I don't know why but I'd never been so sure of anything in my life. Wishful thinking, maybe.

'Who knows the cave's here? Just us. Let's go, okay?'

Like I said, there was enough light to see by, and I very distinctly saw what Ming did as we turned away. Heard him, too. He spat on the Bishop.

I hesitated as he pushed past me and back towards the sunlight. 'That was a bit unnecessary, wasn't it?'

'Yeah. Yeah, it was. Sorry.' Outside the cave he stood up, waded to the bank and took great lungfuls of air. 'Sorry. Pretend I didn't do that, right?'

In the dappled sunlight, blinking, I touched his arm. 'It'll be okay.'

For the first time in ages he looked right at me and smiled a proper Ming-smile. 'Yeah, Cass. Course it will. Listen, can you stay here a minute? You won't be scared?'

'No,' I said. Surprisingly enough it was true. The Thing behind us in the darkness didn't scare me at all. Not now it was dead. That seemed a surprising notion too.

Ming wasn't gone long. When he returned he had a pine branch in one hand and the bloody rock in the other. The rock he pitched into the deepest part of the river; the pine branch he took into the cave. I heard the swish of it over sand as he brushed away our footprints and the long shallow groove the Thing had made as we dragged it. That was good thinking. Cowboys and Indians, I thought. Buried Treasure.

He flung the branch into the river, and with our breath stuck in our throats we watched it drift for a moment. It brushed against a tangle of downswept forest litter, then caught on it, resisting the tug of the current. It stuck there for what felt like a week. Then, abruptly, it was snatched by the current and swallowed, resurfacing ten metres downstream only to race out of sight. I heard Ming start to breathe again, so I did too.

•••

'Listen, Cass, when we walk away? Don't look back.'

'Why?'

'Well, I dunno. Superstition, that's all.'

'Ming! You're not superstitious!'

'No, but…oh, just…Cass, it's just a feeling I've got. Please?'

'Come on, *why?*'

'Don't laugh. Don't. Please. Okay, it's superstitious, but don't look back. When you look back something bad happens. Always. Like Orpheus and Eurydice?'

'Oh, yeah. He's told not to look back but he does. And he loses her forever.'

'Yes. See? You look back, you get dragged down to the world of the dead.'

'Ming, this is so not you.'

'Just this. Just this. Please, Cass.'

'You reeead tooo muuuch.'

'But don't look back.'

'Okay.'

•••

I don't know how poor Orpheus felt, but I've a rough idea. How can you *not* look back? He could see the light. He was out of the cave. He must have thought she was right behind him. The impulse must have been killing him. I always felt sorry for Orpheus, from the day my father first read me the story. It was so unfair. He was almost there. How could he stop himself looking?

And I thought, as I glanced just once over my shoulder: How could I?

5: Maenads

I was on my knees in church the next morning like a good girl, but I didn't stop kneeling even when I was supposed to, which got me a few funny looks from Dad. Fact was, I couldn't get up, my muscles wouldn't let me. I'd slept very well. It was only when I woke up that the memory hit me in the stomach and my blood froze in my veins.

If I was expecting a bit of guidance, a few step-by-step instructions on what on earth I should do next, I was disappointed. God was not at home to Perverters of the Course of Justice. And I could not take my eyes off my father's hands around the chalice as he intoned the words he was paid to intone. I kept seeing them in the basin at home, endlessly scrubbing themselves, over and over, till the lather crept over the edge of the sink.

I didn't want to take communion from him. I didn't want to take communion at all; I was superstitiously afraid I might choke on the wafer. But Mum had already got up and gone to the altar rail, and Dad was eyeing me warily as his fingers fumbled on the paten. A lot of other people were staring too, so eventually I made myself get up on my feet and go forward. I was starting to look like an attention-seeking teenager, when the last thing I wanted was attention. As I sidestepped into the aisle I rubbed my hip as if it hurt. Didn't fool Dad. *Chancer*, his face told me. I got a little scowl, and then a smile.

I liked my Dad a lot. He was lovely, but as I watched

his fingers pick up a wafer that I struggled to swallow, all I could see were those fingers round a rock, crashing it down and down again onto a splintering skull, pulverising the bone, blood splashing onto his hands, Fairy Liquid suds trying to get it off.

When he moved on down the line I had to say *Amen* like Macbeth, only the difference was, I managed it. At the end of the service, I didn't dare look up to see if Dad did or not.

I never liked to look at his face during the final hymn anyway, and today the Warden of Music had picked a chorus Dad particularly hated. They'd banned all the old hymns when they banned Mozart and Stainer and Bach, because even an atheist could love that music. So now we had joyful jolly choruses and chants, and Dad wore a permanently pained expression. You absolutely had to be fervently pious to like One Church music.

I didn't like disturbing Dad afterwards, and I hadn't gone into the vestry for years unless I had to. I found it intimidating. Maybe it was down to growing older, old enough to feel the miasma of religion and politics in the air, discussion and argument and things unsaid, threats unspoken but clearly heard. It was something you couldn't feel when you were little enough to play under the big mahogany conference table. These days the malice and conspiracy hung in the air like a weight pressing down on my head, making it ache, making me want to run from the place whenever I set foot in it. Run, run, not stopping to think, not stopping to look...

But I had to be here because there was something I wanted to ask Dad, and it couldn't wait. Not the obvious thing, of course. That could wait forever.

When I eased open the vestry door he was chatting to his crucifix again, nestled in the palm of his hand, only this time he didn't sound much as if he was pouring out his soul.

'You poor sod,' was all he said. 'What did they do to you, eh?'

Like it was just an old pal, I thought suddenly. Or an imaginary friend, maybe, who used to be more real than anyone. One he'd grown out of, but couldn't quite let go. And my spine went cold as ice.

My Dad couldn't be an apostate. Apostates were lower than unbelievers, lower than atheists. Apostates had renounced their faith, they were traitors, turncoats, heretics. Terrible things happened to apostates.

But I was being stupid. Dad was a One Church cleric, of course he wasn't an apostate.

'Dad?' I said.

He glanced round. For a fleeting moment he seemed shocked, before he smiled at me and his blue eyes lit up. I knew he could make them light up. It wasn't necessarily spontaneous.

I looked around the vestry while he hung up his robes and pulled his jumper over his head. Once upon a time I'd loved it in here: the mushroom-coloured walls, the wood panelling, the shelves full of musty blue hardbacks I couldn't believe anyone had ever read. It smelt of incense and old hymnbooks, bookworm and candle wax. It felt as familiar as the womb, but I wouldn't want to go back there either.

Besides, the room hadn't been the same since the window got broken, the pretty stained glass one. St Michael, I think it was, with creatures and demons and angels around him, all in a little gothic arch that wasn't more than a metre tall. It was amazing the window had survived the first enthusiasm of the militias, and it never was religiously correct. Well, it was gone now. I didn't like the plain opaque replacement glass at all. It made me uneasy. The light that filtered through the leaded lattice was just sunlight, but it seemed cold and brutal after the angel-rainbow that used to spill over the floor, blurred as a half-lost memory. I frowned.

'What's up, Cass?' Dad smiled at me quite gently.

I shook my head and smiled brightly back. 'Okay, this is a stupid question.'

'My favourite kind!'

I laughed, feeling better already. 'What happened to Orpheus in the end?'

'*Who?*'

I rolled my eyes. 'Orpheus, Dad. You know, after he lost Eurydice the second time, what did he do? What became of him?'

He half-laughed. 'Oh, that Orpheus. You don't want to know!'

'Yeah, I do, though. Tell me.'

'Well,' said Dad. 'You asked for it.' Lowering his voice to a growl, he narrowed his eyes to menacing blue slits. 'He gets torn apart by a mob of Maenads.'

'He does?'

'Literally.'

I don't know how I looked but I felt a little green. 'Is that to do with…you know, when he looked back?'

Dad could see I felt a bit sick, so he stopped joking around. 'No, no. Long after that. He spies on the Maenads at their holy rites, and they see him. So they give chase and they catch him and tear him to pieces. But his head became an oracle and Apollo put his lyre among the stars.' Glancing down at the little crucifix, he gave it a rueful knowing glance. 'So that's all right, then.'

I'll tell you now, Dad was right the first time. I didn't want to know.

'Come on, Cass,' he said. 'He's just some priest who falls foul of a bunch of women. Won't be the last.' He wiggled his eyebrows. 'Let's go, I'm starving.'

'Me too.' I turned to smile at him as he put an arm round my shoulders and it was just then that I noticed it. Right beside the bookcase, there was a three-inch dent in the oak panelling. Some attempt had been made to sand it down and revarnish it but there was no hiding the deep damage to the splintered wood. The new stain wasn't the right colour, either. Too dark.

I stopped so suddenly Dad almost tripped, then I put my hand on his chest to hold him back so I could see better. He half-glanced back to see what had caught my attention.

'That's a shame,' I said. 'What did…'

Now, Dad would never deliberately hurt me. He'd never hurt me in my life. I'd had smacks from Mum but never from him; indeed the grumpier old bats in the congregation ascribed the delinquent behaviour of Griffin and me to this well-known fact.

But that was the closest he'd ever come to it, right then. His fingers bit into my arm and he practically yanked me out of the vestry, and I was too shocked even to gasp.

I thought I was in for a row. I thought I'd done something mysterious and terribly wrong, but he just said, 'Lunch,' very brightly, and then he came over all jovial, all the way home. That meant he regretted being so rough but he didn't want to explain, he didn't want me to ask what I'd done wrong. Fine. I was afraid to ask anyway.

Dad, it occurred to me with a shiver, didn't know his own strength.

• • •

He'd left a visible mark and it was going to turn into a spectacular bruise. I had a surreptitious peek while Dad's attention was on the road, under the cover of rearranging my shirt sleeve. He kept taking one hand off the steering wheel and rubbing it across his face and shoving his hair away and glancing sideways at me and sort of hissing through his teeth. Oh, he felt lousy about it. I wondered if I could ask for a pocket money raise on the strength of this.

Then, looking at his tormented face, I thought: No. I don't think I'll mention it again.

There was no point either of us being starving because back home, lunch wasn't even ready. Mum had come home ahead of us, but all she was doing was staring into space, or the cooker hood, I wasn't sure which. Dad immediately forgot I existed. He put an arm around her waist, kissed her cheek and muttered to her. Since she didn't turn round laughing to give him a smooch, I assumed it wasn't sweet nothings.

Somehow I had to take my mind off my grumbling empty stomach. I went through to the television room, where Ming and Griffin were slouched on a sofa passing a can of Coke back and forth as they watched the lunchtime news. I thought it was sport headlines but when I watched more closely I could see the floodlit football stadium was hosting terrorist executions. An apostate: that'd be popular. Second billing: two Jews, a secularist and an Aikenhead. Cheery stuff, not.

'Wow,' I said. 'I didn't know there were any Jews left.'

Needless to say Griff ignored me entirely, but Ming tilted his head right back and grinned at me upside down.

'Hiya, babes.'

'Anything?' I stared at the TV.

Ming's smile switched off and he looked back at the screen. 'Nah.'

I felt bad about being so curt, so I went and leaned on the sofa above him. Since the top of his head was right there and available, it seemed like a good idea to kiss it. Anyway, I liked the smell of his hair. He rolled his head sideways to look up at me. Lifting his hand he raked his fingers once through my cropped hair before reaching out for the Coke can again.

Griff passed it across, but the look he gave Ming was dark, as if he'd like to slap his hand.

'No news at all,' he said sarcastically. 'Unless you count five innocent people getting strung up on live television. Oh, and Martin Kingsmith getting shot in the head.'

'No!' I said. My jaw dropped.

'Yeah, well, Cass meant the Bishop,' put in Ming.

'Who gives a toss about that tosser?' said Griff.

'Martin *Kingsmith* got shot in the *head?*' I goggled at the TV. 'The *film director?*'

'No, Martin Kingsmith, the famous pig farmer.'

'Shut up, Griff. Yeah, Cass, the film director.'

'Is he *dead?*'

'No, he's sitting up in bed eating grapes,' said Griff. 'Of course he's dead, you dolt.'

'Would you quit it? Leave her alone.' Ming didn't often snap at Griff, my brother being older and meaner and one of the undead and everything. How chivalrous, I thought, feeling a flutter below my diaphragm. I glanced down at Ming, all ready to smile my warmest gratitude at him, but he was riveted by the TV again, passing the Coke companionably back to Griffin. 'Look, here comes the Mother of the Nation. Got the onion back in her handbag just in time.'

We watched Ma Baxter walk to the podium. Her eyes were indeed red-rimmed in her doughy face. Usually they twinkled like the eyes of your favourite granny, though the only thing Ma Baxter had in common with our grandmother was that she'd been a single parent abandoned by her feckless husband. Maybe Bunty should have done what Ma Baxter did and turned her personal struggle into a dazzling political campaign – wronged but innocent woman, friend of the poor and pious, tragic but courageous victim of an immoral wastrel: you get the picture. On second thoughts, I don't think Bunty could have pulled it off like Ma Baxter did, with a straight face (and eyes raised devoutly heavenward).

The One Church loved Ma Baxter, informed the electorate she was the strong and pious leader they needed, and let it be known that Hell (or the militias) were a very real prospect for anyone who disagreed. Ten years back, in other words, they handed her the last meaningful election on a collection plate. They were made for each other. Ma Baxter got power and iconic status, the One Church finally got an unshakeable grip on the political process.

I'm not that into politics, but I know all this because my brother never shuts up about it. Neither does my father.

A deal with the devil, he keeps shouting at the poor old radio. *We've done a deal with the devil. And the price is our collective bloody soul.*

And Mum just sighs and goes, *Shush, Gabriel. You'll give yourself an aneurysm.*

Ma Baxter certainly had the last laugh on the feckless husband, found floating past the docks a month after the election with a flick knife between his shoulder blades. A well-deserved flick knife, was the understanding verdict of Ma Baxter's adoring press, and that was the only verdict there ever was, since the only suspect they arrested (a slightly bewildered secularist) was shot in the face by a pious gun nut before he ever got near a courtroom.

Gosh, though, the woman looked good on all that personal tragedy. Her hair was tinted a mousy brown-blonde, but there was just enough grey left at the temples to be reassuring. Between two humongous minders she seemed small and feisty, and their blank eyes and folded arms made her ever so human and endearing in comparison. Not twinkly, though, not right now. She had a tired, grief-stricken air.

'This is a matter of deep personal pain to me,' she was saying as cameras flashed. 'I have spoken to the Commissioner of Police and he assures me his best investigators are studying the CCTV footage. He is as confident as I am that this misguided person will be brought to justice.'

'Misguided,' snorted Griff.

'Sh,' said Ming.

'…I understand fully the deep hurt that Mr Kingsmith caused with his vile film, but this violence was *so* needless.' Sighing, she brushed her forehead with trembling fingers. 'However offensive Mr Kingsmith's visit, however provocative…'

'He came to see his mother!' exploded Griff.

'*Sh!*'

'…should have been safe in our country, and his death is a matter of deepest regret to this government.'

'*How about remorse?*' That came from the TV. The faint shout was only just caught by the microphones, and if the errant journalist said anything else it was drowned out by the shocked muttering of the others, the scrape of chairs as people turned. Of course the cameras didn't turn, but Griff tensed and sat forward on the edge of the sofa, his eyes suddenly alight.

'Blimey, who's that?' said Ming.

'Dunno.'

'Is this live?' I asked, suddenly a lot more interested.

'Yeah,' said Ming, without looking round.

'That'll be Colum Quinn.' Dad was standing at the door. 'Edits the *Questioner*. Writes most of it, too, since there's hardly anybody who'll dare work for him.'

I glanced at him and smiled, but he didn't smile back. He looked very troubled.

Ming and Griff were peering at the screen as if there was

some cat's chance in hell of the cameras focusing on the suicidal loon. Griff shook his head. 'Bet they chop that out for the six o'clock bulletin.'

Ma Baxter's eyes had turned steely, but she recovered quickly and shook her head in the sincerest sadness you could imagine. 'If anyone should feel remorse, it's our neighbours, for provoking this violence! We are a contented, peaceful society, but they'd love to see us riven by conflict and disbelief.' Ma Baxter's eyes were twinkling again, warning and comforting all at once. 'Well, we're a small country, but our Church is a strong one, and so is our faith! Other God-fearing nations stand shoulder to shoulder with us. The United Midwestern States, the Holy African Republic, our allies in the Middle East...'

'She's off,' muttered Griff in disgust. 'What's on the other channel?'

'No, shut up and listen,' said Ming, almost admiringly. 'That was an overt threat.'

Ma Baxter gave us all a direct sweet smile. 'Yes, we believe in dialogue and peace, unlike our enemies. But don't let them imagine we're weak!'

There was a crackling, thumping sound, dull clicks. Somebody grabbing for a microphone, that's what it sounded like.

'Who's actually threatening us, Mrs Baxter?'

Ming laughed in disbelief. 'Whoo! Is he still there? What a trooper!'

'He's a dead man walking, that's what he is.' But Griffin looked hugely impressed.

Ma Baxter had closed her eyes in sorrow, shaking her head as the thuds and shouts grew more distant, ending in a slammed door. 'While we remain strong and sure, we can't be threatened. Not by decadent secularism. Not by split foreign churches that are dying of indifference. Not by North America. And not by the cockroaches next door!'

That was Ma Baxter. Just your rather adorable granny, funny and wise, but then she'd throw in a sentence that made you wonder if you'd heard it right. And of course that made it all the more convincing, because someone so jolly and maternal would never make up that stuff. Someone like that will always have your best interests at heart.

She had her hands clasped together now as if she was praying, her grape-dark eyes lifted heavenwards. 'Thank the One God, we remain united against the true threat: Godlessness! We are under relentless moral and spiritual attack, never forget that!'

A woman journalist raised her pen respectfully. 'Mother Baxter, do you believe Mr Kingsmith's film was part of that spiritual assault?'

'Now, I would never pretend to be a film critic.' Ma Baxter gave a self-deprecating giggle, and there was a ripple of sympathetic laughter from the press corps. 'But let me just say this. If only those who do not share our faith could at least understand and respect it…'

'Oh, that's it.' Griff clicked the mute button on the remote. 'I can't stand any more of her. If it wasn't her militias that shot the poor bugger, I'll eat my PlayStation.'

'Best thing for it,' I muttered.

Griff gave me his worst glare, but Ming was still gazing with fascination at Ma Baxter's moving lips. 'Do you believe in evil, Griff?'

'What d'you mean, believe?' Griff jerked his head at the TV as he stood up and dropped the remote on the sofa. 'It's not a leap of faith. I'm looking at it.'

'Griff,' said Dad, but his voice was so tired it was hardly a warning at all.

'She'll cancel the elections. You wait.'

'Don't be naïve, Griffin,' Dad snapped. 'Of course she'll hold elections. Where's her opposition? Dead, or in prison, or bought off with quangos and junior ministries and crap meaningless jobs. She's neutered us. *All of us.*' He looked as if he might cry. Instead he turned on his heel, slamming out of the room so violently the door bounced back open.

I stared, hoping my jaw wasn't hanging open too far for dignity. Ming and Griff and I glanced at one another, then Griff raised his eyebrows and puffed out a breath. The atmosphere was dense with embarrassment, but with brilliant timing Mum stuck her head round the door.

'Lunch, you three. I hope you're staying, Menzies, I made enough for...'

We all looked round at Mum, but now she was staring past us at the television. As we rose to squeeze past her, she grabbed the remote and clicked the sound back on.

'Too late, Mum, you missed the press conference.' Griff shouted from the hall as he and Ming headed for the kitchen: 'He's dead, shedunnit, come and have lunch.'

Mum only leaned her hands on the back of the sofa as the sleek Tanya Moonfleet smiled at her. 'In regional news, the demolition of the derelict tenements on the East Side finally got underway as Mother Baxter's exciting regeneration plans for the capital come to fruition. The first ambitious phase of development...'

Mum didn't look as if she was seeing anything. She stared at the screen with empty eyes, desolate and sadder than I'd ever seen her.

I blinked and frowned. I'd remembered something very suddenly. Mum leaning on the sofa like that, looking far more cheerful. Must have been a party or a get-together or something, because the room was full of people, and she was leaning on the sofa because Dad was on the other side of it and she was asking him to get her something. Bishop Todd was standing beside her and he turned and put his hand familiarly on her waist, squeezing it. Then his hand swivelled so that his fingertips were actually brushing her backside. Mum didn't like that, and Dad liked it even less, his eyes locked on Todd. Todd was always flirting with Mum, I remembered now, and she'd always pretend she didn't mind, because she had to. Sickeningly I realised what he was doing: insinuating himself, getting close to Griff, covering up what he really wanted.

The memory was astonishingly clear, but the most vivid thing about it wasn't Mum's miserable smile, or Dad's lethal blue eyes. It was Todd's fingers, white and fat and horrible as if they were already the hands of a corpse. Just the memory of them made me shudder, as if I was Mum and those grub fingers were squeezing my waist, touching my backside. It felt so real I shuddered and exclaimed in disgust.

Mum jerked round and stared at me. 'Cassandra,' she said. 'You're still there.'

Jeez. As if it wasn't my house and she wouldn't have expected to find me standing in the TV room. I sighed.

'That's me. Thought you said lunch was ready?'

'Yes, I…' She looked back at the TV, disoriented. Ma Baxter was in a yellow hard hat, charming the demolition workers and getting a chaste kiss on the cheek from one of them.

The reporters were laughing.

'Lunch?' I said patiently. 'Unless that sight just killed your appetite.'

'Lunch,' said Mum, and smiled. No comment.

6: Roadkill

How did it happen? Very, very quickly. So fast you couldn't see it happening.

Why did it? Nobody quite seems to know. Dad says that's because everybody lost interest in politics, just as the One Church was getting very interested indeed.

Here's what Dad tells me, while Mum sighs and puts her hands over her ears and pretends to read a book. That after Church Unity, the One Church just kept swelling like a great big amoeba. They wanted a bigger say in people's lives and the best way to get it was to go straight to the people. Back to basics, back to faith. Back to being the Faithful. And a lot of people liked that. You could believe in the One Church, you could trust it. Not like a bloody politician.

And it was, you know, *catching*.

Dad says: Cass, people wanted certainties. And I'll say, like the world being round? And he'll say, no, not that kind, not the certainties that set you free to ask more questions. *Certain* certainties. Never having to ask yourself hard questions, because somebody already has the answers for you.

So the doubters and the woolly liberals died out or limped off to the neighbouring state to claim theological asylum. If they were slow to do that, or mouthy, or just unlucky, they went missing. Meanwhile graduates were pouring out of the faith colleges and into the Assembly and the Civil

Service and the media, convinced of their ruling destiny (you only had to look at Jeremiah Maclaren) and brimming with political wiles because they'd had extra credits and time off to campaign for the likes of Ma Baxter.

Oh, and all this happened just as the Respect and Privacy Bill was passed, so the media suddenly got terribly wary of offending public figures or insulting religious ones. And it was just like Dad said: people enjoyed having firm guidance again, and the feel of the moral high ground under their feet. Some people were not too happy about the situation, but you'd be amazed how many of them were quite delighted.

So just like that we had a theocratic elected dictatorship. Wham, bam, thank you, Bishop.

I used to say to Dad, well, come on, it couldn't have been that simple. And he'd say, yes, Cass, it really was that simple. It really was that easy.

But he seems bewildered, as if he doesn't understand why he didn't see it coming, and why he ended up on the side he did. I don't know why he did, either. I suppose he had a vocation and he loved his God, and he wanted influence with the One Church, too. And he didn't want to vanish in the small hours or have a terrible accident. And once I heard him say to Mum, I'm human, Brenna. I just am. Venal and greedy and scared and *human*.

• • •

Generally, though, Mum didn't get involved in these discussions because she didn't like to encourage Dad, and she only ever talked politics if she was in a filthy mood. I guess this was one of those times, her hackles almost visibly raised as she scrubbed violently at a pan after lunch.

'Ma Baxter and her schemes. The woman can't afford that stupid bloody redevelopment!' Mum banged the pan so hard onto the worktop I thought she'd dented it. The dishwasher in the corner grumbled and whooshed, so that she had to raise her voice, the tone of it almost hysterical. 'Where does the government find that kind of money?'

'That's the point, Brenna,' said Dad bitterly. 'She'll spend us into an economic crisis to make herself popular. Then she'll whip up the electorate against some poor sods who can't answer back. And she'll blame the neighbours too, of course. She'll have us at war for her bloody vanity.'

They were getting all worked up, and the whole subject bored me to tears since they'd been on about the city redevelopment all through lunch. It was beyond embarrassing, with Ming there and everything. Avoiding more sensitive topics, perhaps, but they didn't need to take it out on the rest of us.

Filching a last chocolate, I raised my eyebrows apologetically at Ming. As I headed for the kitchen door, I heard his chair scrape out behind me. The two of us had set the table, and cleared it afterwards, so it was perfectly fair to walk away even though Griff was stuck by the sink with a dishtowel. Still, the look on my brother's face told me he didn't think the parents should be letting Ming and me wander off together.

Ming caught me up and cornered me in the hall. 'Cass, I need to talk to you.'

He had one hand on the banister and one on the wall, so that his arms were stopping me going anywhere. I gave him a wary look, and he blinked.

'Sorry,' he said, and snatched his hands away, backing off a couple of steps.

My thudding heart calmed a bit. 'So talk.'

'No. Not here.'

'The ghost wood, then,' I said. 'We'll go out.'

He looked over my head, pressing his lips together, then back at me. 'You're joking, aren't you? I don't think I ever want to go back there.'

That's when it hit me for the first time. I realised what we'd done, what we'd corrupted – what I'd corrupted – and I felt an awful swamping sadness. I put my hands over my mouth.

'Ming,' I said. I swore and tears sprang to my eyes.

'Sh, shut up, Cass!' He glanced anxiously towards the kitchen, but we could still hear the clatter of crockery and the relentless political bitching of the parents. 'Don't panic, for crying out loud!'

'I'm not panicking!' I squeaked.

'You bloody are! Cass, *stop it*.' He took hold of my arms, but quite gently. As his fingers tightened I looked down at them, then back up at his face. It struck me that his spots were not that bad; as a matter of fact they were almost gone and you could tell how beautiful he was going to be. That's a strange word to apply to a boy but it's true. I don't want you to think I'm shallow or anything but I'll tell you, he wasn't making me claustrophobic any more.

Almost involuntarily I touched his hair; in fact I took hold of it and pulled his face a bit closer. Then, tentatively, I kissed him. He tasted like Mum's cooking, like home. His mouth was a little cold from the ice in his Coke, but

I was pleased when he stopped being surprised and his tongue caressed mine. I didn't mean to tense up but I did, and I gave another little squeak.

He pulled away. 'Whenever you're ready,' he said, and smiled sweetly.

'Sod,' I said. 'Tease.'

His thumb rubbed my arm manically. 'Cass, we need to talk properly. About…'

'Don't touch her!'

Ming let go of my arms like he'd spotted anthrax spores. Griff was glaring at him, his eyes hard and cold.

'Griff, what d'you think you…' I began, more shocked than angry.

'Talk about what? What do you want to talk to her about?'

'School. That's all, Griff, honest. I need to borrow her notes.'

Why he was indulging Griff's little family-honour routine I couldn't imagine, and I was suddenly furious with both of them. It wasn't as if Griff gave two hoots what I did any more.

Maybe it was just that my chastity was all he had left to be proud about…

Boy, did I feel like a piece of dirt for *that* thought. I felt my ears burn scarlet, and thanked any passing deity that I hadn't spoken it aloud. I swallowed hard.

'You talk to her too much,' said Griff, his eyes still locked on Ming.

Well, that neatly killed off all my guilt and sympathy before it had time to get out of hand. Calling them an unpleasant name – they could draw lots for who it was aimed at – I shoved past the pair of them and barged out of the front door.

I meant to go just to the end of the road, to stand there on my dignity and fume until someone followed and begged my forgiveness. But as soon as I got to the gate I had the most insane urge to turn right, go into the countryside and head for the haunted woods and the river. I'm not the kind of person who fights my urges (which is why my teachers bang on about the peril of my immortal soul) so I lurched unevenly on.

I don't know why I wanted so much to go back to the scene of our… I suppose *crime* is the only thing to call it. It wasn't as if I was mad keen to see the Bishop again. Maybe I was just so angry with Ming I wanted to do something childish and defiant, but I hadn't got halfway to the forestry track when I heard running steps behind me. Ming, rot him, caught me up before I could come to a haughty yet elegant halt. That made standing on my dignity a little tricky, so I kept limping on.

Deliberately I glared ahead and folded my arms as he fell into step beside me.

'Well, don't be mad at me,' he said, when the silence grew uncomfortable.

'Why not?' I snapped. 'Indulging my control freak brother. It'll be honour killings next.'

'Don't exaggerate.' His genuine annoyance gave me a sharp pain below my breastbone. I wasn't used to Ming being cross with me. The irritated-and-slightly-superior role in this relationship was mine. 'He's only looking after you,' he said.

'I don't need looking after. Quit talking down to me.' I

stopped. A car swept past, religious trance music thumping from its open window, and we both took an automatic step back towards the verge.

'Watch your foot,' said Ming, then nipped his lip, as if afraid he'd get his head bitten off for *looking after* me. On the edge of the tarmac was my Disney rabbit, right where I'd left it. I'd nearly put my foot in it. Story of my life.

'Hello,' I told it, then glanced at Ming. He was grinning, his eyebrow eloquently tilted.

'See, talking to dead rabbits is not a good sign.'

I didn't laugh. 'I killed it.'

'Did you?'

'Its spine was broken. A car... a car hit it.'

Maybe I'd looked like that, I thought. Maybe I'd looked helpless and hurt, big Thumper eyes begging to be left alone. Nobody came along and hit my neck with a stick, did they? Sick and dizzy, I put my head in my hands. I wanted to cry, but I couldn't. My eyes and my throat were blocked, my whole head hurt as if my brain had swollen to twice its size and was pressing against my skull. Belated shock.

Back, you voices, back.

'Are you okay? Cass!' Ming's hands were on my head and he was stroking my hair and my temples with his thumbs. He looked so alarmed, his face peering into mine, that I felt better straight away.

'Course I am.' I curled my fingers round his and took them down from my face. I had such an unbearable longing to kiss him, right there on the road, I had to almost fling his hands off mine to avoid making a public trollop of myself. You really didn't want the wrong people to spot you snogging a boy, so I focused on the dead rabbit again, and after a moment Ming did too.

It didn't look much different for its few days as a corpse. Its body sagged in the middle but its fur was intact, right down to its cute little scut of a tail. A line of ants marched officiously back and forth under its belly, though, and it didn't have Thumper eyes any more. It didn't have any eyes. Who was it got his eyes put out because of somebody else's guilty conscience? I'd have to ask Dad.

Or maybe, on second thoughts, not.

I knew Ming was thinking what I was thinking: there was something comforting about that rabbit. Apart from the eyes and the busy little troop of ants nothing had changed. Perhaps there was another corpse not a million miles away that wasn't changing, preserved in its silent cool cave like Tutankhamen. If you didn't think about why the ants were there, and what became of most of Tutankhamen, you might think nothing changed, ever. The rabbit-pelt was sleek and soft, silvery and black-tipped, lifting gently in the breeze. Bishop Todd should have had a fur coat, I thought with a twinge of pity, as a bluebottle buzzed onto the rabbit's empty eye socket.

'It looks fine,' said Ming, 'but when you look underneath there's probably nothing there.'

Suddenly I thought, what if that's how we end up, me and Ming? What if we seemed fine right now but beneath it all everything was rotting and dissolving? He nudged the rabbit's limp back leg with the toe of his boot, distaste in his eyes. What if one day he looked at me with the very same expression? I'd die of it.

No. He was Ming the Merciless, Pirate King of the Galaxy, Commander of the Great Orc Armies of Riverworld, and he was strong and ruthless. A little thing like the illegal concealment of a Very Important Corpse wasn't going to faze him. I rubbed my arms and shivered.

We heard the thump of the car's stereo before we heard its engine. It was coming back towards us, more slowly now, and a muscular arm was leaning on the sill, fingers tapping on the bodywork. It drew to a halt right beside us, so close we should have stepped further against the verge for the sake of our toes. But Ming was staring at the driver's smirking face through the windscreen, and staying resolutely in place, and he wasn't letting me move either, his fingers locked round my arm.

"S'okay,' he muttered without moving his lips.

He didn't actually have to tell me that, and nor did he have to hold onto me. I'd rather lose my toes than move an inch. I folded my arms and curled my lip as the driver leaned out of the window, young and brutishly handsome. He looked even more brutish than usual because there was a dark dry-blood cut on his lip, and an ugly yellowing bruise between his temple and his eye socket, and that eye was very slightly closed. Just as well I hadn't flung myself at Ming.

'Hello, Jeremiah,' I said.

'I thought it was you two,' he said, a slight unpleasant smile twisting his mouth. 'Cassandra and the Minger.'

'Gosh, Jeremiah,' said Ming, deadpan. 'How d'you think them up? No-one's *ever* thought of calling me that before.'

Jeremiah Maclaren's sneer faded, revealing something more frightening in his face that I couldn't quite define. He stared at Ming, then his eyes slewed to me.

'Do up your buttons, tramp.'

I felt Ming's muscles freeze but I found myself involuntarily checking my perfectly modest white shirt. Sure enough, that annoying button had come adrift again. Little *devil*, I thought, irrationally furious with it. I could see the tiny bow at the top of my bra, just peeking out of my practically nonexistent cleavage. So, obviously, could Jeremiah.

I might have been furious with the button but I was even angrier with myself for checking it. Jeremiah didn't intimidate me, I told myself. So why had I let myself look?

Ming turned me towards him. 'Allow me,' he said, but his sweet smile was aimed right at Jeremiah.

Ming gave me a fleeting wink and with slow deliberation, fastened the offending button. His fingertips brushed my ribcage as he did it. Something rippled through my skin and in that moment I hated him. Truly I did.

'You dirty Godless infidel,' began Jeremiah. Opening the car door, he clambered out.

Bishop Todd smiled piously at me from the printed photograph on Jeremiah's t-shirt. The ground beneath me tilted. I stared at the text beneath the photo, trying to get my composure back. *Our anger is righteous, our motives are holy.*

Ming's grin was becoming a rictus. 'On your own again, Jeremiah?' He peered past him into the empty car, his teeth now clenched into that ferocious smile. 'Want some more?' Brusquely he let go of me and turned to face Jeremiah.

They eyed one another, but I took a breath, because Jeremiah had nearly put his foot in my rabbit. He must have noticed my movement because he followed my gaze.

Taking a step back, he deliberately placed his heel over the rabbit's eyeless head and crushed it, grinding it into the tarmac. As I watched it crumple, I felt sick. With most of my brain I knew the rabbit couldn't feel it. But in another small part of my mind I winced.

'Watch yourself, Minger,' said Jeremiah, very softly.

He climbed back into the car and gunned the engine. The car squealed away, its tyres kicking up dust.

'Jerk,' said Ming, when the car was gone and the scream of protesting gears had faded.

'Damn right you are,' I yelled, shoving him away.

He was so shocked he stumbled back and nearly fell. 'Cass…'

'Don't use me as a prop in your little power games,' I snarled.

'That wasn't… I… ' Recognition and remorse dawned on his face. 'I didn't mean to, Cass. Really. I'm sorry.'

He knew he'd gone too far and he *was* sorry, but I was too angry to forgive him right then. And it's hard to explain, but I was upset about my rabbit. I couldn't look at it or at him as I clutched my shirt – the button having popped again – and ran away from him down the road.

'Cass!' he yelled.

I turned, running awkwardly backwards for a few steps. I felt an awful twinge in my hip and half-stumbled, but I teetered and kept my balance.

'Sod off, Ming,' I yelled. The harder I yelled, the easier it was not to cry. 'Just *sod off*.'

Oh, my hip hurt. But even though I was listing badly, I

ran. I kept on running so that he wouldn't try to catch up, so that he'd know with perfect clarity that I didn't want him to.

• • •

That night I dreamed I was in the vestry. I stood there on the worn rug, delighted, because my old angel-rainbow was back, spilt across the floor by summer sunlight. I looked up at the window but of course the stained-glass wasn't back at all. The plain ugly leaded panes were still there, but St Michael himself was outside and he was all the colours of the rainbow. He was so beautiful, him and his jewel-coloured angel-face, but his expression was twisted with terror, his mouth open in a silent scream, and he was hammering hard on the glass. I wanted to let him in but I was too afraid, I was afraid that pack of howling Maenads would burst in behind him. I put my hands over my face so I wouldn't see his desperate terror, so I wouldn't see him as they dragged him down. Their faces were masks of hate. One of them was Mum. She grabbed St Michael by the hair and tore him to the ground but I could still hear his fists hammering, hammering on the glass. I crouched on the floor with my arms over my head but Maenad-Mum shouted for me. *Get up, Cass! Get up!*

'Get up! You're late, Cass!'

And I blinked and opened my eyes, just before they ripped him apart.

7: Looking For Clues

The vestry was locked, but what's the point having a One Church cleric for a father if you haven't got the nous to know where he keeps his keys? My heart was slamming so hard as I pushed open the vestry door I thought it would fracture a rib. If Dad caught me he'd be cross, but after losing it yesterday he'd be treading on eggshells where I was concerned, and I'd just have to hope nobody else walked in. I didn't even have an excuse lined up, since I couldn't think of one. My only plan was not to get caught.

What was I looking for? I didn't even know that myself. Something was niggling at me, that was all.

A lot of things were niggling at me. So many things they'd ganged up and turned into a permanent headache. But the vestry seemed as good a place as any to start. What happened to Griff had happened here, I was sure of it. I felt surrounded by ghosts, and I shivered.

It was so gloomy I had to fight an impulse to turn on the lights. I was afraid to look at the diamond-paned window in case a rainbow-face started hammering on it and screaming, but when I did look, of course there was nothing there: just the dull distorted grey of the clouds through a latticed prism of glass. I chewed my lip. The window was recessed deep into its gothic arch and I couldn't think how someone had managed to break it. You'd almost think it was deliberate except that no-one would dare vandalise a church, not with the religious militias prowling the streets. And I knew it had been broken from the inside because months afterwards I'd still been finding shards of glass in the flowerbed outside, the light gone out of them as if they'd died.

Dad used to have this staple metaphor for his sermons: stained glass was like his religion. He said if you were standing outside it looked meaningless and dull, obscuring everything. If you'd just walk inside you'd see the colours and the beauty and the whole picture and the sense it made. Standing there on the inside, I wondered who'd look into the light and see the beautiful elaborate design, then want to shatter it into a million pieces.

Well, the window was gone and it was only ever going to come back to me in horrible dreams about mob killings of archangels. And Dad had not preached about stained glass for a while. He hadn't talked about much except injustice and corruption and a lapdog media, ranting on till half the congregation began to wriggle and mutter and the other half sat with their faces frozen in fear for themselves, and maybe for him too.

I frowned as I ran my forefinger across the dented panelling, feeling the roughness where splinters had been sanded down. Something stirred at the back of my brain, something tried to scramble out of the clamour, so for once, instead of beating it back down, I shut my eyes to concentrate. No. Reaching for the thought made it slip away like a fish. I stared up at the light fitting above the mahogany table where the Wardens held their meetings, then at the tops of the bookcases. Up there were stacked old papers and broken books and boxes that no-one would ever need to see again.

Gripping the back of one of the mahogany chairs, I dragged it across to the bookshelves. I could get one arm up on top if I stood on tiptoe and hung onto the shelves with my other hand, so that's what I did, fumbling around, finding little but dust and dead spiders. So long as I didn't find a live one, I'd be fine. I wished I hadn't decided to do this, but now that I was here, now that I'd started, it'd be stupid to give up. At least I'd be able to tell myself I had a look, I tried, there was nothing there, so *don't worry about it*. Clambering down off the chair, I shifted it another couple of feet, blowing cobwebby dust out of my eyes and reaching up yet again. This was *really* stupid. Carrying on, I decided, was actually stupider than giving up.

That was when I found a Live One. I upended a shoebox and must have stuck my hand right in Shelob's Lair, because eight repulsive feet stalked across the back of it.

I gave a strangled shriek. It was a big one. Instinctively I jerked my hand sideways, because I didn't want to pull the beast down onto my face, and my fingers banged into something hard and metal. When I'd shaken off Shelob I pulled my hand down, my heart crashing, and rubbed my knuckles. I whimpered quietly. Not because my fingers were hurt: because I was mortally afraid someone had heard me, and because I'm not very good with spiders.

Now it really was time to stop. I stood there on the chair, shaking, sucking my knuckles, tasting blood. I couldn't put my hand up there again. I just couldn't. Gripping the bookshelves with the tips of my fingers, I leaned back and peered upwards as if there was the remotest chance of being able to see.

It must have gone. *It's more scared of you than you are*

of it. It's more scared of you...

I pulled a couple of books and a *Cruden's Concordance* off the shelf, piled them on my chair and balanced on them, pulling myself a little higher with my fingertips and craning my neck. Then, moaning through tightly-clamped lips, I thrust my hand up and flailed for the metal thing. I missed, but felt it smooth and cold against my hand. At my second grab I got hold of it, stumbled off the chair, and stood there clutching my prize against my chest, eyes shut, breath wheezing in my chest.

I'm going to have to get therapy about the spider thing.

When my blood stopped pounding in my temples and I still hadn't died of heart failure, I opened my eyes and gazed at the object in my hands. I knew right away what it was: the sheared-off base of a silver candlestick. It was stained and tarnished, and there was a slight dent in it. Right in the middle of the upper side was a black hole, a little rough at the edges, where the actual stick had once been soldered on. Of course it would break there quite cleanly. But only if it hit something *very* hard.

The base was hideously Victorian, embellished with curlicues and flourishes. Holding it in both hands, I looked back up at the top of the bookcase, chewing my cheek. No. The rest of the candlestick must be up there, but I wasn't going to get it. Uh-uh.

Reverend Green. In the Library. With the Candlestick...

No, no, no. There weren't any bloodstains on it, for a start.

(Okay, you could wash them off...)

And Dad wasn't likely to go into the woods with a ruddy great silver candlestick in his jacket pocket.

(Unless it was premeditated…)

Alternatively, he was hardly likely to commit bloody murder in the vestry, then drag a Bishop's overfed corpse through the streets and into the countryside.

(Unless he could get him in the car boot without anyone seeing…)

I swallowed hard. What had all my nosing around achieved, apart from some bloody knuckles and a terrible worsening fear? I looked back at the broken weapon in my hands. *No*. At the perfectly innocent *candlestick base*. The sheared-off bit was black with tarnish, and the whole thing had a thick layer of dust. I drew loops on it with my forefinger, and it came away furry with grime. Yes, it had been up there for ages. I sagged with relief.

As I glanced back upwards, wondering if I could safely toss the thing back there without dislodging several cardboard boxes and a large cross spider, I caught sight of the dent in the panelling that had brought me here. Catching my lower lip in my teeth, I held the candlestick base against it. It was just about the right size.

I pressed the edge of it into the dent, adjusting the angle. It was just about the right shape, too.

Once more I ran my fingers across the dent, then, feeling daft, I leaned down and sniffed. It wasn't remotely tacky and there was no chemical smell. It hadn't been done recently.

Okay, I was going to stop wasting my time now. The Bishop had been killed with a *rock*: I'd seen his blood and brains all over it. Besides, what kind of a hiding place was the vestry for a murder weapon? It wasn't as if Ma Baxter's entire police force was pathologically scared of spiders. This was just my overactive imagination again, getting me into trouble. For crying out loud, I thought, as reality cleared my brain and gave me a sharp jab in the conscience, I was going to have some explaining to do if a Warden walked in.

At any rate, I wasn't climbing back up there. I counted to three – okay, make it five – said an automatic inward prayer and drew my hand back for a gentle underarm toss.

At which point the door flew open and I dropped the thing.

Griffin was the colour of bleached parchment. 'What are you doing?'

Stupidly I looked at the candlestick base on the floor, so Griff did too. He paled even more, and his ears went red as I stooped to pick it up.

'What's that? Why have you got that? What the *hell* are you doing in here?' As he barked all these questions, giving me no space to answer them, he was grabbing for the thing in my hand. I panicked, stumbled back and lifted the candlestick base warningly before I knew what I was doing. Instantly he backed off, blinking and shoving his hands into his hair.

Breathing hard, we stared at each other.

'Put that down,' he snapped at last.

What was I thinking? I tried to put it carefully on the table, but I let go of it so fast it clattered down, probably leaving another dent. Griff jumped.

'Are you crazy?' he whispered. 'What are you doing here?'

'I was looking for something.' I was whispering too. It was infectious.

'What?' said Griff warily. 'What were you looking for?'

'Answers? I don't know. Answers, that's all.'

'Don't do that, Cass. Just don't.' Griff's expression was unreadable.

I thought: he's scared. He's just scared, for all his cynical cool, for all his violent games and his teenage politics. He's not Young Byron and he's not The Shadow or The Crow or the Dark Knight of Gotham City. He's my brother like he was before and he's scared, and I don't blame him. I felt an almost unbearable affection for him.

'Griff,' I said, and scuffed the carpet with one foot. 'Can you just tell me if you…'

'If I what?'

'I mean, just if you want to tell me? Anything. You know?'

'Such as?' His tones were getting increasingly clipped but I felt I owed it to him to say it.

'Anything you want,' I mumbled. 'That's all. If you need to.'

I could feel his stare branding my scalp. He was silent for so long I couldn't bear it any longer, I had to look at him, even though blood had rushed into my face and my cheeks stung. I raised my head and met his eyes.

My brother looked angry enough to kill me.

I don't know what we'd have ended up saying to each other, but luckily we didn't get the chance. Distantly, but coming closer, someone was singing *Suspicious Minds*. Griff was still watching me, but his expression softened a little, almost as if he might laugh. I was so hugely relieved I could have kissed Aunt Abby.

Abby had quite a good singing voice, but not when she

was wearing her iPod. She knew all the words of course, but she must have had the volume turned up too high to hear herself, because she was well off-key. As she pushed open the vestry door, she stopped singing.

I shuffled guiltily. Griff gave me one warning glare, then turned to his favourite aunt and kissed her cheek. 'Hello,' he said. 'D'you know you're singing out loud? He's banned, Aunt Abby. Watch yourself.'

'Don't soft-soap me, Griffin,' said Abby briskly, tugging out her earphones and tucking them into her pocket. 'What are you two doing in here?'

'I'm keeping an eye on *her*,' said Griff in a tone that made me feel like something under a rock. He was all cosy and conspiratorial, as if expecting Abby's unqualified support. 'She keeps sneaking off with Menzies.'

'And?' said Abby.

I had another urge to kiss her, but Griff went pale again. '*And* Dad's keys were missing. That'd look great, wouldn't it? A rector's daughter with the son of a secularist, right in her father's church, having a snog.' He added viciously, 'Or worse.'

'Yeah,' I snapped. 'That wouldn't look too good. Could get me in a lot of trouble if that was actually what I was *doing*.'

'I can't help noticing, Griffin,' said Abby as she thumbed the controls of her iPod and turned it off, 'that you also know where your father's keys are kept.'

'That's because I used to serve at the altar,' he pointed out sullenly.

'Well,' said Abby, 'you can stop acting the One Church acolyte now, dear.'

Griff's ears went scarlet. 'I'm not…'

'Ah, Griffin. God loves you and so do I, but if you don't get your backside out of my presence I'll leather it for you.'

There was nothing he could say to that, so with a final warning glower in my direction he stalked out. His footsteps echoed down the aisle, clattering disrespectfully on the tiles; Abby's little dart had obviously struck home. Then, distantly, the outer door slammed.

I had my teeth clenched, waiting for my own lashing from Abby's legendary tongue, but all she said was, 'Oh, Cassandra, you daft cow. Look as if you're doing something constructive.'

She bent to rummage in a cupboard, pulling out the polishing kit. Selecting a couple of random items from the silver cabinet, she dumped them on the table.

'We won't bother with that, though.' Taking the candlestick base out of my unresisting hands, she climbed onto my chair and stowed it back on top of the bookcase. God, her skirt was short. At her age, too. Just as well her brother-in-law was a One Church cleric, though I still didn't know how she got away with it, and she wasn't doing Dad any good.

Dusting her hands cheerfully, she jumped down, then pulled out a chair, patted the neighbouring one, and began to smear Silvo on a chalice.

Stunned, I slumped down beside her. She had the tip of her tongue between her teeth as she wrapped her forefinger in a yellow duster and rubbed at a patch of tarnish. Like Mum, Abby was still very pretty. Big hazel eyes like Mum's, too, but she didn't have all the freckles dusted across her nose, and her hair was redder than Mum's and mine, as befitted the scarlet woman of the family. Ours was more chestnut. Hers was more L'Oreal, especially that fiery shade on the ends. She'd got all the boob genes, too, lucky woman, and as I glanced enviously at her cleavage I could feel myself pulling my shoulders back to jut out my flat chest a bit more.

'Ah, why don't you grow your hair again, Cassie?' said Abby the family telepath.

'Why?'

Her fingers froze on the chalice. She sucked her teeth, as if afraid she'd spoken out of turn. Funny, that, since I was used to being on the receiving end of Abby's unsolicited opinions.

Into the silence, I gave an exaggerated sigh. 'Yeah, let me guess. Boys like long hair.'

Recovering, Abby grinned. 'Menzies would. He's a nice boy, Cassie.'

'Not you too,' I groaned. 'He's my *friend*, Aunt Abby.'

'He *used* to be your friend, Cassandra.' She reached for my hand and turned it over, examining my wrist with a critical eye as she pressed her fingertip against a vein. 'Friends don't make your pulse speed up like that.'

I snatched my hand away, then stared down at the blue veins under thin pale skin. They seemed horribly vulnerable and fragile but you couldn't actually see a heartbeat. What did she have, superpowers?

'Don't be too hard on Griff,' I said. Hah. Take that, Abby! Smooth change of subject.

'Why not?' Her voice was clipped. 'He's got no right to police your behaviour.'

'But...' I squirmed. 'It's sort of understandable. Isn't it?'

'Why is it understandable, Cassie?' She raised one tawny eyebrow (oh, the hair was definitely tinted), but her fingers were furiously busy with the yellow duster. I picked one up too, and grabbed a small candleholder, just for something to occupy me.

I chickened out. 'He's my big brother, that's all. Aren't they all like that?'

'No,' said Abby. 'And he should be letting you make your own mistakes.'

'What happened wasn't his mistake!' I blurted.

Abby's hand slowed and stilled on the silver. Anxiously she searched my face, but I concentrated hard on my little candleholder. I liked it. It was small and plain and unassuming. It would take nothing bigger than a tealight. I liked it much better than those great ornate Victorian candlesticks that were made so big and imposing just to make you feel even smaller than you were. The kind you could do real damage with, if you lifted one and...

I shuddered and stared at Abby, who had something like panic in her expression. 'Something happened in here,' I said. 'Didn't it? Something happened to Griff.'

And I was here. The realisation hit me so hard I lost my breath. *I saw what happened.*

Abby managed to close her jaw, just. Carefully she put down her chalice and her duster, then took hold of my wrists so hard it almost hurt. I bet she could feel my racing pulse now.

'You listen to me, Cassie,' she said intently. 'If anything happened – and I do mean *if* – if anything happened to anyone anywhere, it's in the past. It's not going to un-happen. There's nothing can be done and there's nothing to be gained by stirring it up. Now I know that goes against your popular bloody wisdom, Cassandra, but it is *true*. Do you understand me?'

'Yes,' I said. I didn't agree. But I understood, all right.

'Your brother does not need to protect you, do you hear me? You are a strong girl. You can look after yourself. You can protect yourself, for God's sake! All right?'

'Yeah, all right.'

'Your protection is not his business!'

'*All right*,' I snapped. She was making me nervous now with her killer glare.

Abby pursed her lips and blew gently. 'Oh, sorry, Cass-ie. Griff's fine, you know. He's all right. It's just that these things can get out of hand. You don't want to end up down the Laundries scrubbing cassocks till you're fifty so the boys can't get their hands on you.'

'Yeah, like my Dad's going to let that happen.'

'Things can happen without anyone wanting them. One thing follows another and before you know it you're on the high road to Hell. I nearly ended up in those sweat-shops, but Bunty stood up to her rector. Thrashing me was her job, she told him. Heh!' Abby smiled to herself. 'Ah, don't let those religious nuts get you down, Cassie. He's a nice boy, your Menzies.'

'Oh, for God's sake,' I said crossly.

Killer glare again. I turned away sheepishly.

'Don't take the One Lord's name in vain, Cassandra.'

I stopped being sheepish, and let my jaw drop.

'I'm a God-fearing thirty-nine-year-old, young lady, and you're all of fifteen,' Abby told me primly, and with a touch of smugness. 'So don't look at me like that. You don't have to respect the One Church but you'd better show a little respect for your Maker or he'll be asking all kinds of awkward questions later.'

Thirty-nine, I thought dryly. Aye, five years ago, maybe. 'And I'll be telling *him* I don't think much of his top-down managerial skills, seeing as his organisation's got a bit out of hand.'

'No blasphemy, Cassandra, please. A little respect. The Church is a living compromise, and it wasn't easily done.' She sighed. 'Ah, the One Church can't last forever, that's what I think. Too many stresses and strains. One day it'll disintegrate. Then we'll be fighting sectarian wars again, killing each other instead of the infidels.'

'At least atheists won't tell us how to behave.' I was warming to this. I'd had quite enough of it from Griff, so it fairly tripped off the tongue and I was glad to be firing it at someone else. 'Secularists won't tell us how to run our lives.'

'Course they will.' Abby winked at me. 'Look at the mad ones, blowing themselves up when they don't even have a Heaven to go to. There's dedication for you.' She gave an eloquent snort. 'Oh, we should all be minding our own business. Finding our own happiness and letting other people get on with finding theirs. You, for instance, my darling. You can start in your own little way by…'

'Letting you throw me at Ming.' I rolled my eyes. 'Uh-huh. I saw that one coming.'

'Away and go on. Throw yourself. He's lovely.'

'Way too lovely. He's *so* up himself. He's already mess-ing me about, Aunt Abby. He'll get fed up with me and then we won't even be friends any more.'

'Uh-huh, and this is the boy you've known all your life, is it?' said Abby scornfully. 'Don't let your pride get so big you can't see over it.'

I couldn't get the candleholder any cleaner. In a minute it would be suffering serious erosion. Reluctantly, with blackened fingers, I set it down.

'Now, I know what you're thinking. You're thinking, who's Abby to be lecturing me on my love life? Seeing as hers has been such a resounding success.'

She had that right. She had it so right my cheekbones burned with embarrassment. I picked black out from under my fingernails, hoping she was going to change the subject in the near future, or leave, or be struck dumb by her (so far) incredibly tolerant Maker.

'See, Cassie, the aggravating thing about adults is our patronising reluctance to let you make the same mistakes we did.'

Indeed, and to accuse your big brother of just that, less than five minutes ago. *Griff*, I thought, *come back! Come back and rescue me from the madwoman and you can boss me around as much as you like! LOOK AFTER ME!*

'See, when it comes to love,' said Abby, scraping somebody's Twelve-Hour Lipstick off the chalice rim with a fingernail, 'saving face is not a priority.'

Actually my immediate priority was to get out of there. I started to wriggle in my chair.

'Sit still and shut up and listen to the only lecture I'm ever going to give you. I've watched you and that boy. He might not be the one for you forever, but right now he is. I know it's tempting to save face, but you can live without your pride. You can't live without a heartbeat. Sometimes you need to take a risk, Cassandra.'

Oh, God, I thought, blanching. If you only knew...

But she was getting into her stride now. 'I knew this boy when I was young. Handsome, but very kind eyes, and that's an unusual combination.' Abby sighed nostalgically. 'Well, I liked him, but he wasn't going to break my heart. Oh, no, no-one was going to make a fool of *me*. So after we'd flirted a bit I sent him a little note, but I didn't sign it, and I thought, if he guesses it's from me, this'll be the beginning of something.

'And he did guess, Cassie. But he only went and asked me, asked right out if the note came from me, and of course I panicked and denied it. Just in case he was taking the mickey, you know? Just in case he'd be laughing about it later with his pals. I denied it very convincingly; oh, I was a great liar when my pride was at stake. So nothing ever came of it. I could have loved that boy.' Her eyes had a faraway look. 'Ah, I had my pride, though, Cassie. My dignity was intact, and much use may it be to me when I'm cold in my grave.'

I stood up sharply. I'd actually found that quite sad, and I felt for her, but right now *cold in my grave* was not a phrase I wanted to hear, even if, strictly speaking, the Bishop wasn't. 'Aunt Abby, I need to go,' I said desperately.

There was a wounded look in her eyes that cut me to the bone. 'Well,' she said curtly. 'Give me those keys. I'll clear up. I'll have to tell your father but I promise he won't be angry.'

'I know.' I nibbled my thumbnail. 'All right. Thanks.' Laying the keys carefully by her hand, I hesitated. The woman had just opened her heart to me and all I could do was run away. Feeling guilty, I tried to make a joke of it. 'What brought this on, anyway?'

She breathed on the chalice and rubbed it with her sleeve, then checked her own lipstick in the reflection. 'Things turn up, Cassie.'

That observation made me feel sick. 'What?'

She tweaked the corner of her mouth with a coral fingernail. 'I mean, things happen. People have to go away. Whatever. I've been meaning to tell you my one-and-only nugget of wisdom since your father was pouring font water on your screaming bald head and I was promising to be a good godmother. Well, I haven't been. So that's the hottest tip I can give you and it may not be much use to you but I thought I'd get it in while I had the chance.'

I was alarmed now. 'You're not ill, are you?'

'God, no! What gave you that idea? I'd just hate you to think I was going to be around bugging the backside off you for all eternity. Well, I will, but that's in the next world.' She laughed. 'Nobody's around forever in this one, that's all. So remember what I said.'

'I will.' Funnily enough I meant it, because she'd scared the daylights out of me there. I gave her a quick tight hug, which surprised her no end. 'Thanks for that. Honest. But I need to go.' I fumbled for an excuse she'd appreciate, and fortunately my flash of inspiration came at that moment, rather than two hours too late as usual. 'I said I'd meet Ming.'

'Ah.' Sure enough, her eyes lit up with vicarious lust. 'You run along then. And remember double what I said.'

'Uh-huh.' I smiled at her, and backed out still smiling. And then I made a run for it.

Bad Faith

• • •

I was so relieved to be away from there, away from Aunt Abby and her tart-with-a-heart monologue, that it was a genuine shock when I woke up at three a.m. replaying the whole stupid thing in my head. What was all that about? Why had she brought it up now? What did she mean, *People have to go away* and *I'm not going to be around for all eternity*? And how come things can seem of such minor importance in the daylight, and tie your gut in knots in the small hours?

I lay watching the digital glow of my clock count down the minutes till dawn, longing to go back to sleep. I thought about Aunt Abby and her lost love and for a while it wiped out all thoughts of Ming and even of Griffin. For about five minutes it seemed like just the saddest thing I'd ever heard in my life, and I spent four of the five minutes crying buckets into my pillow. That's three a.m. for you.

It wasn't like Aunt Abby was an expert on violent death and the concealment of bodies, I thought, and that's where some advice would really have come in handy.

God. If I'd only known, I could just have asked.

8: Jaw Jaw

'Hey, Cripple,' said a voice behind me. 'Where's your Infidel?'

Grinning, I turned. 'Hi, Ruth. Suspended again, the big eejit.'

'You better look after that boy or I'll be taking him off your hands.' She winked at me.

At Ruth's back was the usual straggle of wannabe-rebels and hangers-on. Mostly girls, but there was one sallow dark-haired boy with bright nervous eyes who seemed to regard Ruth as his personal saviour and bodyguard. I didn't quite get it because he wasn't her type, but she can't have minded his company because he was attached to her by invisible elastic.

We'd been running between Moral Studies and Maths, a quick changeover, and we weren't supposed to talk in the corridors. Not in loud voices, anyway. It was considered disrespectful to the teachers and to the One God. Rose Parsons must have felt we weren't showing sufficient respect, because she tightened her pious pretty mouth as she passed us, then spoilt the effect by throwing a truly filthy look over her shoulder.

Chewing hard on her gum, Ruth hitched up her bag and gave Rose the finger.

'Self-righteous little cow,' she sniffed. 'Wish I'd killed her when I had the chance.'

I giggled, couldn't help it. 'You never had a chance.

Don't talk such mince.'

'I can dream.' Ruth gave me a brilliant smile. 'Really, Legless. Poor old Minger. You don't look after that Infidel, I'll have him. *Cute*.'

She was a mouthy girl, Ruth, and she was going to get in a lot of trouble one day, but until then: get her alone, or in her small trusted coterie, and she was a hoot. People like her made school bearable and I hoped they weren't going to die out.

That hope – carelessly worded – gave me a sick feeling in my stomach. Things weren't so bad. Everybody knew the authorities would loosen up a bit soon, because things couldn't continue at the same radical fever-pitch forever. I was uncomfortably aware that there was another side to that ropey theory, which was that things always got a lot worse before they got better, but I shoved the thought away, sent it to join the rest of the low-key cacophony in my brain. One more thing I didn't want to think about.

'Go and give us some gum.' I kept an eye out for Dr deVilliers as Ruth pressed a stick of gum into my hand. Cruella considered chewing gum the work of the devil, along with so much else (including my Macbeth essay, which had not gone down well. I wondered what Dad would say when he saw my D minus. I hoped he'd think it was funny).

'You're okay, Legless.' Ruth shoved her remaining gum into her pocket. 'For a sky pilot's brat.'

'Sh,' I said. 'Shut up. Hurry up and all. I don't want another detention. My dad's okay, and don't call them that. You'll get in trouble.'

'I could call them a lot worse. I was only polite cause it's your dad.' She sniffed again.

'Just watch yourself,' I warned her.

It was something people said a lot. *Watch yourself. Watch your mouth.* It wasn't aggressive: it was caring, it showed concern. We all did have to watch ourselves. Because other people undoubtedly did.

Ruth was no saint: she was an out-and-out bully when she could get away with it, and she used to think it was fun to bully me, when I was still limping badly. She bullied me even though I was a 'sky pilot's brat', and for that I had to admire her nerve. Later, though, she had a change of heart, me having whacked her shin with a crutch and left her wordless and gasping with agony in a corner of the toilets. After that she decided I was under her protection. I'd have liked to be her friend, too, but politically that would have been stupid, and there was no future in it. I had Dad to think of, and let's face it, Ming was bad enough. I'd known Ming since before I was toilet-trained, since the world was young and his parents were wealthy landowners and dinosaurs ruled the earth (or would have done, if we were allowed to mention evolution). Ming was different, Ming was a special case, but I couldn't afford any more inconvenient friends. Ruth, when she hit what passed for the real world, would have to shift for herself.

Right now she could still intimidate her way out of trouble. She had her small gang of rebels, she could defy the world because she was strong and brassy and brave, and I was happy for her.

'So,' she said now. 'What news of the old goat Todd?'

I blinked. The crazy cow could still shock me. An adult could hang for a remark like that. Opening my mouth reflexively to remonstrate with her, I remembered Griff. Poor Griff. She was right: Todd was evil and devious. One of these days I'd know what to do about it. But the low clamour in my head wouldn't let me think straight, not right now. 'He's a... he's a...'

'Goat,' Ruth said again, helpfully. 'Filthy old goat. Made my flesh creep at assembly. Squeezing the girls' bums when he got the chance. Leering at their tits. Old goat. See you.'

I laughed, shocked beyond speech. But I felt superior, too, with my secret baleful knowledge of Todd's true crime, and now I only needed to know what I'd do to make things right again for Griff. I loved him, but in the last few years I didn't know him any more. That was down to Todd. So Todd should be punished. Something must be done.

Except that something had already been done. The memory jabbed me in the gut. Something *had* been done, finally and fatally.

Amazing, isn't it, what the mind can wilfully forget? As I watched Ruth swan into Maths ahead of me, arrogant and unhurried, I thought about Todd's bloated corpse, float-ing into the cave like a fat canoe, and wondered what I'd already wilfully forgotten.

• • •

Ming was waiting for me outside the school gates that af-ternoon, which I thought was needlessly provocative to Jeremiah and the rest of the Scripture Corps. Even I wasn't sure if I was pleased to see him. A train of thought was winding tortuously through my head: something I was trying to remember, something I'd said to him in the wood, something vital that I couldn't quite grasp. When I saw Ming, the train of thought left without me.

As I stopped and smiled nervously at him, Esther Kelly shoved past and pulled out her mobile. Walking backwards, she kept her eye on us as she thumbed a speed-dial button, her weasel-pretty features twisted into a smirk.

'You've done it now.' I made a face at Ming. 'Jeremiah won't be on his own this time.'

'Nope. He won't make that mistake again.' Ming grinned. 'Let's get out of here.'

We got out of there. Ming was pretty good with the murkier alleyways of town and I felt perfectly safe within about ten minutes. I felt even safer when he casually took hold of my hand. Lordy, I was turning into a simpering wuss. I'd be in an Empire-line dress before I knew it.

'So what did you want to talk about?' I asked him at last.

His fingers tightened on mine. 'What do you think? What else have we got to talk about?'

That made me cross. 'You seriously think that's all we'll be talking about for the rest of our lives?'

'Er,' said Ming, nonplussed, and I realised what I'd said.

I swallowed and tried to fight back the blush. This, as everyone knows, only makes you go redder. 'I mean, presuming we're going to be friends beyond next Tuesday or whatever. Just friends. Obviously.' Jeez, I was making it worse.

'Obviously,' he said, glancing to left and right, then back at me. A muscle under his eye twitched, and he lifted his hand to touch my lips.

That was worse than being kissed, worse than his hands running down my back: just that light pressure of his fingers against the corner of my mouth. There was a gremlin in my ribcage, merrily putting my heart through a wringer, and my innards were pounding like a bellyful of pistons. You might call it a rush of blood to anywhere but your head.

Making the effort of my life, I managed not to kiss his fingers. Or suck them, or flaming well eat them, along with the rest of him. Holy hormones.

Ming slewed his eyes away so that he wasn't quite looking at me. I could see his heartbeat in his throat. His fingers slid away from my mouth and the back of them brushed my cheek, then came to rest against my ear.

Determined not to squeak and give myself away, I looked levelly at him.

'Cass, don't worry about the... the cave,' he blurted. 'That's all I wanted to tell you.'

'Don't worry,' I echoed stupidly. 'Right.'

'Because if you worry... if you think about it too much – you'll start... oh, I dunno. Saying things, maybe. Being nervous. Giving yourself away.'

'Giving *us* away,' I corrected him, hoping with hindsight that didn't sound like another threat.

If it did, he didn't let on. 'Yes. We don't want to behave any different. Nothing strange.'

I thought our behaviour was a little weird right now, but it was nothing to do with the cave and its contents. The nerve endings in my ear were behaving extremely strangely. And the rest of me. 'How many murder stories have you read?' I asked him. ''Cause if you ask me, all they've done is make *you* nervous.'

'That's not murder stories,' he said. 'That's you.'

He flexed his fingers so that the tips of them rested lightly behind my ear. Nice. Then he used his tenuous hold to pull me closer, and kissed me again. Nicer.

I didn't want to stop kissing him, and I got the distinct impression he didn't want to stop either. It was quickly out of our hands, though.

'Hello, *Cassandra*. Hello, Minger.'

'Bugger,' said Ming softly.

As we turned to look at Jeremiah, I saw a fleeting fear cross the big thug's features. I knew where it came from. The overused nickname had slipped out automatically and now he was afraid Ming was going to mock him again, in front of his three hulking pals and two sneering girls. That was what scared Jeremiah Maclaren, I thought: laughter. But glancing at Ming's curled lip, I knew he wouldn't mock Jeremiah for that, not again. Unlike *some*, I thought with fierce pride, Ming wasn't sad enough to recycle a joke.

Neither of us spoke. We just watched them.

'You've got some nerve, Minger, hanging round the school.' Jeremiah's swagger was back. 'Education's for the Faithful, not infidels. Keep on showing up, though. I want an excuse to deal with you.'

'You and who else?'

I thought that was a mighty stupid question, seeing as Jeremiah had five cronies with him right now, but I avoided kicking Ming's ankle and kept my lip zipped.

'The militias, Minger. You think your parents are safe, in a funny way, don't you? Because the cops are always watching them?' He smiled. 'We've sympathisers in the police force, Minger. We've *members* in the police. But we're not inhuman, even to Godless dissidents. We wouldn't like to leave you an orphan.' Jeremiah smiled again, more nastily. 'So when we've finished with them, we'll come for you. All right?'

I knew Ming wanted to say something cheeky and defiant, but it must have stuck in his throat. A small shiver ran across his skin.

'Look at the pair of you.' Jeremiah sniggered. 'What a waste of Intelligent Design. Why didn't your fathers give you decent religious names?'

'Cassandra's a religious name,' said Ming. 'Just not your religion, you pig-ignorant dick.'

Okay, that was asking for it. And he got it. They piled right in on him. And on me: oh, cheers, Ming, I thought, while I was still thinking rationally.

Now, I'm quite small, and I'm skinny (and not in a nice way), but if Esther Kelly and Rose Parsons thought I wasn't going to put up a fight they had another think coming. I'd be far happier breaking Esther's neck than I was breaking my rabbit's, so I was hardly going to hold back on the teeth and the fists. After all, I wasn't without scrapping experience, seeing as I grew up with a slightly older brother, so I held my own for a bit.

Ming, though, had four of them against him. When Esther was curled on the ground, temporarily winded by my foot, and I was straddling Rose with my hands round her neck, I risked a quick glance in his direction. He was not having a great time of it but the yelps and grunts weren't only coming from him. Something really struck me then, even harder than Esther kicked me as she recovered and got me off her pal.

Talk about Ming the Merciless. I was astonished at how ruthless he was. He didn't hold back at all, but went for eyes and throats and groins with incredible savagery. Obviously that only made them come back at him with double the ferocity, but still, he'd done a respectable amount of damage by the time two of them were managing to hold him down while the others put the boot in.

Esther had her arm round my throat now, dragging me down. 'Stop,' I managed to gasp. 'They'll kill him!'

'So? You too, bitch.' That was when Rose made the mistake of flinging herself on top of me.

I don't know what happened then. I went a bit demented, that's all. Rose had long blonde hair and I *knew* that was a big misjudgement on her part, and I knew exactly what to do with it, too. I grabbed a hank of it, ripping it from her scalp till she squealed so loud Esther had to let go of my throat to try to wrestle my hands off her. Not a chance. I was so mad at Rose I dragged her over, shoved her face down in the road and scrambled onto her back, ignoring Esther's yells and her pummelling fists and tearing nails. I had a pretty good grip, so I tore Rose's head back and slammed her jaw into the tarmac. I didn't so much hear the jarring crunch: I felt it.

Esther screamed. Rose just made an awful gurgling moaning sound. The four boys dropped Ming, who curled up foetally, and goggled at Rose. And then there were running footsteps and furious shouts, and the gang panicked. Jeremiah and one of the others picked up Rose between them and they half-ran, half-staggered off, throwing curses back in our direction.

I flung myself down beside Ming, dying to touch him and scared to. What if his skull was fractured, what if his neck was broken, what if I...

He opened one swollen eye and grinned. 'Bloody hell, Cass.' His voice grated in his throat and he couldn't quite get the words out right, so he spat some blood and a chunk of tooth, and tried again. 'Bloody hell. Y'okay?'

'I'm fine, I'm fine, don't move, I...'

Somebody grabbed me from behind. He'd have come to the same grief as Rose Parsons if he hadn't remembered to shout: 'Cass! Cassie!'

With a surge of joy I recognised Dad's voice. Then he was slumping down onto the pavement and hauling me backwards into his arms. That felt nice. I wouldn't have abandoned Ming for anyone else, but I tell you, that felt nice. And safe. I let my head loll back against his familiar chest. 'Hi, Dad,' I mumbled.

Dad's old drinking crony Wilfred Makunga was halfway down the street in the gang's wake, obviously straight out of church since he was still in his billowing cassock, and he was standing there shaking his not inconsiderable fists and bellowing, *'You shits! You filthy little shits! I KNOW YOUR PARENTS!'* at the top of his booming voice. Not very ecclesiastical.

I stared at Ming, my thoughts tumbling around my spinning head. 'You're ruthless.'

One of his eyes was already half-closed and purpling. 'Look who's talking,' he said.

It hit me then, what I'd done. In an instant I was sick and terrified and my whole body felt like one big bruise. I didn't take my eyes off Ming's, but I didn't dislodge Dad's arms, either. 'I'm in trouble, Dad,' I whispered.

'Jesus, Cass. No kidding.'

'No, I mean *trouble* trouble. I think I broke her jaw.'

My gentle peaceable Dad hugged me fiercely. 'Good,' he said.

9: Bodies

I ached to see Ming, but they wouldn't let me. Not because he was hurt, and that was what infuriated me: because *I* was, and allegedly they didn't want me hurt any more.

For God's sake, Cass, look at the state of you. That was Mum. *Just keep your head down for a while. Please. Please, love.*

The best thing you can do for him is stay away from him. Dad was fiercer and colder than I'd ever have expected, his eyes steel-blue. *Wilf got him medical attention, if that makes you feel better. Ming's damn lucky, so keep his luck good. Stay away from him, Cass.*

My brother was more predictable. *Don't let me find you near that idiot or I'll finish what Jeremiah started.*

And the maddening thing is, I felt so guilty about reducing Mum to tears and Dad to moral blackmail, I went along with it.

I'd stopped sleeping, though. The fight had shaken something in my head, and like a can of Coke thrown at a wall, the contents wanted out. If someone didn't snap the ring pull soon I was going to explode. Never mind the cacophony, I *knew* there was something recent I had to remember, something about that day in the wood. It felt like the most important thing in my life and I had to remember it for Ming's sake, but there was so much rage and old confusion jumbled up in my brain, I couldn't find it. I lay awake every night crying with frustration but I couldn't pin it down.

Despite Wilfred's mouthy threats, Jeremiah's gang didn't get into trouble, not one of them. Ming's suspension was turned into permanent expulsion: well, so much for his medical career. I got one concession for having the bejaysus beaten out of me, and I think I only got that because Rose Parsons did, too, and because after all my father was a One Church cleric: the school let me sit my exams at home. I was amazed at their lenience. Certainly it must have seemed amazingly lenient to Dr DeVilliers, who sat there invigilating me as if it was some kind of martyrdom. Cruella had a soft spot for Rose Parsons, I remembered, so that can't have helped, and nor could the fact that Rose was meant to be her Titania in *A Midsummer Night's Dream* in a week's time. The old bat glared at me for two hours at a stretch, purse-lipped, and between her Evil Eye and my own inward distractions, I performed dreadfully on every paper.

I didn't care. I was lovesick and guilty and terribly frightened, I was dazed with insomnia, and I kept thinking: well, Ming isn't sitting exams at all and he never will. If I'd been smarter I'd have taken the attitude that I was disproportionately lucky and ought to make the most of my own opportunities, but I wasn't thinking that way. I was barely thinking at all.

The exams must have preoccupied me more than I thought, though, because the logjam in my brain cleared, unexpectedly, the morning after the last one. Or perhaps I'd stopped hunting consciously for my lost thought, and that's why it sneaked back of its own accord.

And woke me up with a hard slap in the face.

• • •

I don't know why Mum wasted money on breakfast cereal. Dad ate on his feet every morning, stuffing a slice of toast into his face and mainlining coffee while he watched the news. Griff, as far as I knew, had barely eaten human food in about three years. Drank the blood of bats overnight, or something, and he didn't look good on it. And Mum's appetite these days was about the same as mine. That morning we hid from each other on opposite sides of a giant carton of Rice Krispies, and we had nothing to say.

On reflection, maybe that's why mothers buy cereal: for the boxes. They give you something to read when the awkward silence becomes unbearable.

I'd been staring at that carton for a while and I knew the vitamin-and-mineral content off by heart, not to mention the names of every character in that god-awful new animated movie *Rodent Rapture!* I hoped I wasn't going to get the free plastic angel hamster falling into my bowl: it'd feel like a dreadful omen. Reduced to studying the barcode, I almost wished for another exam, something to learn by rote, something enlightening to read. There was nothing but a yawning gap in my brain and my heart. The summer loomed in front of me, empty, dark and awful: Mingless.

Panicking, I shovelled Rice Krispies into my mouth, forcing myself to chew, tasting only dust. The radio burbled in the background: more PR puff about the redevelopment in the capital, more outside-broadcast demolition sounds as high-rises collapsed or wrecking balls crashed into crumbling tenement walls. And more meaningless banter from

Ma Baxter, boring on about her economic ambitions for her beloved nation. Mum had stopped even pretending to eat. The fingers of both hands were twisted into her hair as she stared at her plate.

It occurred to me that Mum had been brought up in those tenements, and maybe she was sad about her entire childhood imploding in clouds of dust. Well, so what? Metaphorically speaking my childhood had just done the same, and frankly I had no pity to spare for anyone beyond myself and Ming.

To keep from seeing the misery in Mum's eyes, I stared fixedly at the Rice Krispies barcode. It didn't take me long to think it reminded me of something. Something I'd seen quite recently on the Internet, over Griff's shoulder.

Then I connected.

I jumped out of my chair like a scalded cat and slammed out of the front door. With Mum's stunned cry echoing in my ears, I ran hell-for-leather for the woods, and the river, and the cave.

• • •

It was hot, so hot. It had to be one of the hottest days of the year. June can be like that, of course, before July and August kick in with the rain. Looking back, it seems so predictable, but maybe that's hindsight. Like everything else.

I kept worrying about the heat every time I broke into a painful jog, every time I limped to a walk. Sweat trickled down my spine, made my underarms sticky and blurred my eyes. Oh, God, what would the Bishop be like after four weeks in May and June, trapped in that cave? Cold in his grave? Hardly.

I felt sick and I wanted to cry, but I didn't have time and I couldn't spare the energy. I didn't even know what I could do about the godawful mess we'd made. But I had to try.

We'd pulled the Bishop out of the water. He was lying in a cave, high and dry and perfectly findable, I knew that now. And on his cassock, or maybe even on his arm, was Ming's perfectly identifiable saliva.

Godless Darwinism might be something we didn't mention, but that didn't stop the government making use of science. That Rice Krispies barcode jiggled and danced before my eyes as I stumbled down the forestry track and into the woods, black and white stripes that wobbled mockingly into a DNA code. All the animated characters from *Rodent Rapture!* were pointing at it and holding their sides and laughing their little bug-eyed heads off at us. Oh, God, how could we have been so stupid? *How could Ming?*

I had to slow my pace as the hill steepened. Spiders landed on my arms and face and chest, with no Ming to break the webs for me, but I had to keep going. Half the time I had my eyes shut, but even when they were open I tripped on fallen branches camouflaged by overgrown moss and lichen. My t-shirt was wet with sweat now and – oh, God, there was another, clinging to my shoulder, so I swiped it off with a yelp – and my hip just ached. I was going to suffer for this tonight, I knew it. Another sleepless one. So what?

Tiny sticky legs on my face. I yowled, then realised I

was panicking. Calm down, I shouted inwardly, don't be pathetic, it's only a bloody spider, there's something a lot worse waiting for you in that cave.

Except it was worse even than I thought. As I scrambled down the slope and came in sight of the riverbend, dread turned me cold and hot sweat stung my eyes, and I had to grab a pine branch or I'd have fallen. Because something was *coming out of the cave.*

I stopped. So did my heart. I thought I'd faint; maybe it was just the heat that was making my brain swell till I thought my boggling eyes would pop out of my head.

The figure waded ashore and stood up straight: young and lanky, I realised, breathing again. Too much hair for a zombie Bishop. He dusted his hands together, rubbed them on his jeans, twisted them, flicked away something invisible, and finally stooped to plunge them back into the river. He crouched there for ages, letting the water flow over his hands right up to his wrists, then submerged his arms up to his elbows. Rising shakily to his feet he turned, and his eyes met mine. They were hollow and miserable and scared, and they were still bruised.

'Cass,' said Ming.

His voice was very faint, but I heard him clearly in the hot stillness of the wood. The birds were too drowsy to sing and even the river hardly made any sound, its waters brown and calm and rippling.

I limped down the last bit of slope to his side, but he backed away and flung up a hand. 'Don't touch me,' he whispered.

I could hardly get the word out. 'Why?'

'Because I smell of... I had to touch the...' His eyes were

glazed and very green in the forest light. We stood there in silence for an age, and then we both said it together.

'DNA.'

Ming gave a huffing laugh, then we were both talking over each other.

'When did you…'

'I didn't think…'

'I remembered. This morning. It just hit me, Cass. I can't believe I was so stupid.'

'See?' I managed to smile at him. 'I knew we were psychic.'

I made a half-hearted attempt to go towards the cave, but Ming stood in the way. 'Don't go in there. Please.' The hollowness was back in his blackened eyes. 'Please don't. I've done it.'

I was very shocked, though I'd been planning to do it myself. But I was hugely relieved, too, that I didn't have to go in there and scrub off the stain. As ever, Ming was my fall guy.

'Do you think you…' I began.

'I don't know. I don't know if I got it off. I don't care. I did my best.' There was a greenish tinge to his skin now, too, but it might have been the hot light through the summer foliage. 'It doesn't matter. I'm not going back in there, I'm not.'

'Of course you're not,' I soothed.

'We lugged him all the way down here. We'll have left traces all over him!'

'Yeah. I know, but *that*…' I shrugged and fell silent. Ming must feel bad enough already. No need to say it: that you might be able to explain a lot of things, forensic technicians might even miss a lot of things. But not a great gob of spittle.

'There's something else.'

'What?' My mouth dried.

Ming swallowed. Then he gulped again, and again, as if his throat just wouldn't let him speak. At last he took a high-pitched breath.

'Somebody's been in the cave.'

All I could do was stare. I didn't want to ask how he knew. I didn't want to hear about footprints in the sand. *I didn't want to know*. It was like my exam results: an envelope I wasn't going to open. I clamped my mouth shut and stared at Ming, shaking.

Ming dragged his t-shirt off over his head, then turned his back on me to fumble at his belt and the zip of his jeans. Then he was shoving past me and half-running upriver, along the little rabbit-path and down to the pool under the cliff, where a long underwater rock formed a natural weir. Sitting down on the rough sand, he tugged off his trainers and stripped off his jeans and underpants, then staggered gratefully into the water. With a great shuddering breath he sank under the still surface.

Running after him, I skidded to a halt on the tiny beach and gaped, completely thrown. Along with the frisson I got from seeing him buck-naked, I couldn't help feeling a bit sidelined. He hadn't stripped off for me, I thought resentfully: he'd stripped off for the Bishop.

That struck me as funny. And it was hot, and I was dizzy with relief that I didn't have to go into the cave. Besides, I was just hysterically happy to see Ming again, whatever the circumstances. Those were my excuses for starting to laugh, and I was still laughing helplessly when Ming's head resurfaced, his hair darkest blond and plastered across his shocked eyes.

I couldn't stop laughing. He watched me as if I'd taken leave of my senses, then ducked back under. When he came up he fired a mouthful of water that got me right in the face.

That was even funnier, but at least it made me cough so much I had to stop laughing. Flicking his hair out of his eyes, he grinned at me.

'C'mon in,' he said. 'The water's lovely.'

'Liar,' I told him. But I stripped off anyway.

After all, what was that old rope swing for? It needed testing, after a whole year's neglect. Some kid might venture down here, and try it out, and get hurt when it broke. I had a moral duty…

Ah, but the rope had survived just fine, I thought, whooping as I swung out over the pool, let go, and plunged into the water, drenching Ming again.

I loved the river in its summer mood. It was cold enough to knock the air from your lungs, but you got used to it in seconds, and then you felt you could stay there forever. I wished we could. We were getting a bit old for horseplay and duckings and splashings, but what the heck, we indulged ourselves. Even the Bishop might have heard the screams and yells.

Quite a bit later, but almost simultaneously, as if at some signal only bats and teenagers could hear, we snapped out of the riotous mood. Contented silence fell between us. I shut my eyes to see the flicker of tree shadows against my eyelids, and floated blissfully onto my back. Bumping into

Ming, I half-floundered, limbs flailing and splashing, but calmly he slipped his arms under mine and clasped his hands across my chest.

'Shush,' he said, in a perfectly normal voice. 'Relax.'

Happy again, I drifted in the gentle pull of the river, my shoulders against Ming's chest, his chin resting on my head. The river was cool on our pleasantly numb limbs, the sun hot on our heads. I could lie here in Ming's arms indefinitely, and he seemed content with the arrangement. We were breaking all kinds of laws, and if anyone saw us we'd be in such deep trouble we'd never talk ourselves out of it, but no-one was going to see us. There was a rotting corpse in a cave just a little downstream, but even he seemed an almost benevolent presence. We were getting used to him. *He didn't scare me any more...*

The sun drifted briefly behind a sliver of cloud and I shivered. Shaking himself, Ming kissed my cropped hair and let me go.

I couldn't help being disappointed as he splashed to the tiny rough beach. 'I'm not cold,' I said, trying not to sound petulant.

'That's how people get exposure,' he told me darkly. Flinging his clothes into the river he waded after them, then scrubbed and wrung them out, over and over again. Speaking of exposure, I was getting a good view of Ming now, but he seemed too distracted to worry about it.

'You'll have to get home in those.' I nodded at his clothes.

He glanced up at me through wet strands of hair and shrugged. 'I'll wait till they're dry.'

Goody, I thought. So will I, then.

When he had hung his things on handy tree branches and perched his trainers on a sunny rock – he'd even washed those – he didn't come back in the river, but sat down in a mossy hollow between the river and the trees, where the sun blazed full on his pale body. Scrambling out of the water to join him, I knew he was watching me very intently, though he was trying not to show it and there was a slight blush on his cheekbones. I let myself stare back. Most of the cuts and bruises were fading, but there was still a big black-and-yellow stain across his cracked ribs and in my head I kept replaying the horrible sight and sound of Jeremiah's boot going in. A tingle of hatred went down my spine.

'You okay?' I asked him.

'Yeah.' He shut his eyes and lay back, flopping one arm out to the side in what I chose to read as an invitation. He certainly didn't object when I slumped down beside him. The arm went round my shoulders and I curled happily against him. He gave that funny huffing laugh again.

'What?'

'Nothing. Trying to picture your brother's face.'

'Yow. Don't do that.' I laughed into his shoulder, then shut my eyes and inhaled. He didn't smell of anything evil. He smelt of river and sunlight and moss.

'Is Griff very angry?'

I hesitated. 'They all are,' I said at last. 'But I don't think they're really angry with you.'

'I bet they are,' he said. When I opened my eyes he was gazing at the sky through the dipping branches, sunlight dappling his face. 'I'm really sorry about it, Cass.'

'It wasn't your fault.' *I love you*, I thought.

'I need to thank your dad's pal. For getting me in to see a doctor.' He rubbed a tooth ruefully with his free hand. 'And a dentist.'

When anyone mentioned Wilfred all I could think of was what he said to Dad that day as he gripped his arms, shaking him to calm him down. *You'll get it back, Gabriel. You will get it back.* Wilf had muttered the words quickly in the empty echoing alleyway, as if afraid the church building itself would overhear. *He won't leave you forever. I know He won't.*

Even in the hot sun, I shivered at the memory. Ming's arm tightened around me.

'I don't think we've heard the end of it,' I said. 'Cause of Rose. That's my fault.'

'No,' he said. 'Don't worry.'

'Uh-huh.' *I love you.*

'It'll be okay,' he lied. He smiled slightly. 'This makes up for your birthday.'

'Mm?'

'We didn't get to swim on your birthday. Because of the floods.'

'Oh. That's right, we didn't.' We always swam here on my birthday, every year. It was always just warm enough by the middle of May, or it was if you were a Pirate Queen with something to prove to your brother and your male best friend about female equality.

'Remember last year?' Ming's eyes were shut but he was grinning. 'Damn, that was cold. And the time before that? You were turning blue but you wouldn't come out 'cause Griff had hidden your clothes.'

'Yeah! The pig!' *I love you.*

'D'you remember when you were eleven? And Griff found that frog and…'

'No,' I said. My eyes flickered open and my smile faded. I frowned. 'No, I don't remember that.'

He stared up into the pine branches. As they shifted against the dazzle of light, they made shadow patterns across his eyes so that I couldn't quite read them. 'Maybe it wasn't that year.'

'I don't remember the frog. At all.'

'Right.' His arm tightened again, his fingers squeezed my arm and his mouth twisted into a half-smile. 'I wouldn't remember it, if I was you. Wipe the whole thing. Oh, the trauma!'

I giggled. 'Okay. Take your word for it.'

He was silent for a while. At last he said drowsily, 'You been sleeping?'

'No,' I murmured.

'Me either. Go to sleep now, then.'

I do love you. I snuggled closer into his naked body, letting his warmth seep into me along with the sunlight. 'Too chivalrous, you.'

'M-hm.' His eyelids drooped heavily. 'Not superhuman, though. Go to sleep.'

He didn't have to tell me three times. I went to sleep.

• • •

We woke shivering, clutched tightly against each other in an unconscious search for shared warmth. No time to revel in it, though. Pushing me away, Ming grabbed up his watch and peered at it, and swore; I leaped to my feet and

started snatching his clothes from the branches and toss-
ing them to him, then seized my own. We dressed without
looking at each other, our backs decorously turned, which
would have struck me as funny if I hadn't been in a blue
panic.

The sun had disappeared, and there was a grey chill to
the breeze. Big droplets of rain spattered onto our skin.

That's the end.

The thought came to me out of nowhere, and made me
shudder. The end of what? Summer, innocence, my childhood? Not me and Ming. Please God, not me and Ming.

'Come on.' He took my hand, and I could feel the
warmth of his blood. He gave me a knowing grin. 'If you
promise to try and run, I promise I'll take the spiders.'

10: It Runs in the Family

I'd expected Mum to confront me in the hall, because I'd missed supper by hours and she took that extremely seriously (*What do you kids think, I cook this stuff for myself?*), but there was no sign of her or anyone else. My clothes were drenched again, but with rain, not sweat. Ming needn't have bothered waiting till his were dry; when he left me he was already soaked through, and he had another couple of miles to walk.

I was glad he had waited, though. I think he was, too.

In the house, the ominous silence was almost tangible, so that the only sound finally filtering through to my ears was like something rubbing and squeaking against the silence itself. It took me a moment to realise it was someone wielding a J-cloth in the downstairs bathroom. Well, that explained the unfamiliarity. Mum hated cleaning the bath.

The sound stopped, and it didn't restart. I pushed open the door. Mum was kneeling on the floor beside the tub, her back to me, but she stiffened and straightened slightly as she felt my presence. The bathroom reeked of cleaner, lemony and chemical, as if she'd used a whole bottle of the stuff. She drew a hand down her face, then stared at her rubber glove as if its texture on her skin was a shock, as if she'd just remembered where she was and what she was doing.

'Cass,' she said, without looking round. 'Where have you been?'

'A walk,' I mumbled.

'I was worried.' It sounded automatic. Mum didn't sound all that worried, just distracted, and despite chafing at all her recent fussing, I could almost feel offended. Now that I thought about it, there was no smell of cooking in the place. What, hadn't I even missed supper, then?

Even when I edged to her side, she only stared into the bath. I glanced over her shoulder. Oh, okay. A big black spider, squatting at the bottom of the tub just where it curved upwards. She'd cleaned all around it, though she'd given it a wide berth: I could see the streaks. Lying close to the spider was a plastic tumbler, right where Mum had dropped it, presumably having failed to catch the brute first time.

Amazing, isn't it? The things that run in families.

'Can you not just kill it?' I said.

Mum didn't dismiss the suggestion out of hand. Briefly she glanced up at me, her eyes troubled, then watched the monster, which didn't look remotely nervous. Sometimes they did, like they knew what was coming, but not this one. It was glaring at us with eyes that were out on stalks, and if it could have put its hands on its eight little hips it would have. Mum's fingers trembled as she snatched up the tumbler. Holding it on its side, she let it hover briefly over the spider, but shut her eyes as she slammed it down. Hopeless. Missed by a mile, but at least the thing had now scuttled into the middle of the bath, and was a decent target.

Feeling sorry for Mum, and not remotely sorry for the spider, I picked up Dad's paperback that was sitting beside the loo, and dropped it from a height. The invertebrate crunch was a minuscule echo of Rose Parsons's jaw. Bullseye.

We both watched the book for an edgy minute, as if eight tiny arms were going to prise it off and chuck it back at us, like a cartoon spider. At last I took the cover between thumb and forefinger and picked it up, turning it so we could see. Splat. For the first time I noticed what Dad had been reading: James Patterson, *Along Came A Spider*. I couldn't help giggling.

'What could be more appropriate?' I said.

'*Charlotte's Web?*' Mum laughed too, a little breathily.

I was just relieved to see her smile. 'I was never keen on that book.'

'I wonder why?' Mum tilted an ironic eyebrow at me. 'Where were you, Cass?'

'I told you. A walk.'

She paused for a heartbeat. 'Did you see Ming?'

I hesitated too. But I didn't want to lie to her. I scuffed the bathmat with my toe. 'Yeah.'

She didn't react like I thought she would. All she said, dully, was, 'Be careful, love.' Then she leaned on the bath, rested her folded arms on the edge of it and pressed her forehead to her arms with a sigh that made her whole body sag.

'Mum,' I whispered. 'What's wrong?'

She turned her head sideways but she didn't have the energy to get it off her arms. Her eyes met mine, and I thought for a scary moment there were tears in them.

'They found a body, Cass.'

• • •

About five light years later, I found my voice.

'They can't have!' I yelled.

I suppose Mum had every reason to be stunned. She lifted her head from her arms and stared at me. 'What?'

'They can't have,' I moaned. 'No. They didn't have time!'

Mum got to her feet, stooping because she was still holding the edge of the bath. My Mum, my beautiful laughing relatively-young Mum, looked for a terrible two seconds like a broken old woman. Then she stood up properly.

'What are you talking about?' There was bewilderment in her face, and a dawning suspicion. Mum was getting her composure back, along with whatever else had deserted her this afternoon. 'What's the matter with you, Cassandra?'

Ah. Clearly this required the fastest regrouping I've ever achieved in my big-mouthed life. Wide-eyed, I stared back at her, and tried not to eat my entire lower lip.

'*Angels and Martyrs*. Isn't that what you're on about? Did they find Theresa's body under the patio?' I swallowed hard, wondering if I was pulling this off. It didn't feel like it, so I gave a hearty little laugh to reinforce my act. 'Mu-um! I didn't know you were a daytime TV junkie!'

She did not look convinced, but clearly there was too much on her mind already.

'It's not that, Cass.' She twisted her J-cloth between her fists, her eyes red and glistening.

'What, then?'

'It's Holy Joe. Holy Joe.'

'*What?*'

She'd lost me. For a bewildered instant I didn't even

know who she meant: it was so outrageously out of context, and he belonged in lurid bargain paperbacks in tourist shops, and the old psycho was before my time anyway. I shook myself, sighed in exasperation. He was gone, he hadn't killed anyone in twenty years, they couldn't have found another body, and even if they had they'd never admit it, they'd cover it up and sneak him back into whatever lunatic asylum he'd escaped from. What did Holy Joe have to do with anything, besides a tenuous, delicious family connection that used to get me all kinds of oohs and aahs in the playground?

The J-cloth ripped in two pieces, one in each of Mum's hands. Now she was entirely immobile. The house was so silent you could have cut the air with a blunt knife, but I couldn't hear her breathing. After dragging seconds, she broke the stillness with a desperate little gasp.

'They found Holy Joe, Cass. Aunt Abby's been arrested.'

And then my mother burst into tears.

11: Surfacing

What with Dad having been at the police station all day with Wilfred, trying futilely to get some kind of access to Abby, I thought the house was empty apart from me and Mum. Outside, the relentless wetting drizzle had turned into a rainstorm, battering against the window panes and hissing and dripping eerily down the unlit chimneys. I suppose that's why I didn't hear the sound effects of Griff's PlayStation, but I did smell the cigarette smoke as I passed his room.

Hesitantly, I knocked. No reply, not even an injunction to piss off. I took his reticence as an invitation. My shock was beginning to turn into comforting anger, even at Mum, who couldn't explain herself coherently, and who had finally shut herself into the bathroom and me out of it. I shoved open Griff's door with my foot.

He knew I was there, but he didn't say a word, his thumbs prodding manically at his console. The atmosphere of stale smoke and bitterness made me faintly nauseous. Griff's window was open and rain gusted in, steadily dampening the magazines and papers on his desk, but he wasn't taking any notice, and it was having no effect on the tarry miasma. Just beside his right hand a cigarette smouldered in an ashtray, but God knew when he last took a drag on it, because there were two inches of frail ash still attached to the filter. His bony shoulders were hunched and as I stood behind him I had an impulse to put my hands on them and squeeze them, comfortingly. That was one impulse I resisted.

His screen flashed a message at both of us. *QUIT GAME?*

'Griff, what's happening?'

He shifted in his seat and began again.

'All I want,' I said, 'is somebody to tell me what's going on.' I added bitterly, 'For once.'

His shoulders moved. It might have been a shrug. We stood in silence till he got killed again, and it didn't take long. He was rubbish at these things. *QUIT GAME?*

'What's going on?' I said.

RESUME.

'Why's Abby been arrested?'

A plastic-faced CGI priest turned his crucifix on Griff.

QUIT GAME?

'Griff – '

He spun his chair and screamed at me. 'I don't know! Can't you see I sometimes don't know any more than you do?'

'Sometimes,' I echoed dully.

'Yeah! Sometimes! I don't know what's going on, okay? I'm in the dark here! You think Mum's snapped out of her funk long enough to tell me? They're coming to question her later, did you know that? The bloody police are going to know the story long before we do.'

I took a step back, horrified. Tears were burning at the corners of his eyes and now one leaked down his cheek. Griff rubbed his hands fiercely across his face. 'This is Todd's fault, that's all I know. None of this would have happened if it hadn't been for him. We'd be *normal*. Well, he's dead and I'm glad.'

Silence fell, except for a howling gust of rain against the window. Griff blinked, glanced at it, then turned and slammed the sash down, shutting out rain and wind and the outside world. The room seemed even more oppressive now. I wanted to say, *How do you know he's dead?* But where would that take us? What would be the point?

'He must be dead,' Griff mumbled. 'He'd have come back by now.'

The screen behind him blinked insistently. *QUIT GAME?* He must have caught sight of it, or its reflection, because with an air of unbearable irritation he turned and yanked out the lead, and the screen went blank.

'That's not good for it,' I said, stupidly.

'I know, I know.'

I took a deep breath that sounded like a gasp. 'So do I,' I blurted.

His forehead creased with confusion. 'What?' he said. 'What d'you know? About Abby?'

'No,' I said. 'Not Abby. Todd. I know about Bishop Todd.'

I stared at Griff's feet. Guilt churned in my stomach, but this was my business, it *was*. I'd been in the vestry that day. I'd seen what happened. I needed to tug the memory out of the jumble in my head and take a good look at it, though I didn't want to. I'd seen it once and I didn't want to see it again. What would I do if I saw such a thing?

Griff had said absolutely nothing. When I looked up the tips of his ears had gone red.

'You don't know anything,' he said at last.

'I do.'

'No. No, you don't.' There was horror in his face.

'I don't mean about him disappearing. It's not that I...' I hesitated, my eyes narrowing. 'Do you know anything about that?'

There, I'd asked, and I felt like a small piece of river scum, possibly scum from a rotting corpse. Griff didn't take his eyes off me but he shook his head slowly.

It wasn't the most convincing denial I'd ever seen but for me, it would do. 'Right.'

He licked his lips nervously. 'What d'you think you know?'

Another deep breath. 'You and Todd. That's what I know. What happened between you and Todd.'

He gave a small gasping laugh. 'You don't know anything,' he repeated, and laughed again. This time I could hear its desperate edge.

'I saw it,' I said. '*I saw what he did!*'

'No. Cass. No, no, no.'

'You don't have to lie to me!' I screamed, enraged beyond tact. 'Everybody else does but you don't have to!' I wanted to hit him, and I must have tried, because suddenly his arm came up, and with shock in his eyes he deflected my fist and caught hold of my wrist. 'I know what he did, so don't keep shutting me out. It wasn't your fault!'

If Griff was not entirely white, he was certainly Hint of Magnolia. Lordy, even his ears had paled.

'Why are you ashamed, Griff? There's nothing to be ashamed of!' I knew I was going too far now but I was terrified of what he was going to say when I finally shut up, so I had to keep babbling on. 'It was his fault! He's the one who did wrong. He abused *you!*'

Oh, shit.

We just stood there. My wrist was still in Griff's hand, my knuckles white from being clenched so tightly, but suddenly he let it go as if I'd burned his fingers. For a horrible moment I thought he was going to hit me back. Then I saw it: Secret Identity Griff looking out through Dark Griff's eyes. And now I was scared. Now I really was.

'What did I do?' I shouted.

'You didn't... you didn't...'

'I know what he did to you, Griff. *What have I done to him?*'

Griff touched my cheek with his fingertips. 'Cassie,' he said in a shaky voice.

He was going to tell me then, I knew it. So I jerked away from him and ran out, slamming the door so hard it shook in its frame. I'd thought I wanted to know; now I was terrified he might tell me. I ran till I'd put as much distance between me and my brother as my small part of Planet Earth would afford.

12: Waking

I wandered in a daze. I knew where I was going but I didn't care how long I took to get there, because my mind needed some filing work. The shaken-Coke-can feeling in my head hadn't left with my DNA revelation. I needed to defragment my brain.

Griff was upset. That wasn't entirely my fault, I told myself, sick with remorse. I couldn't have been any clumsier, the way I'd spilt his horrible secret, but it wasn't just that. His misery was about Abby, too. Griff adored Abby. But he could hardly blame Todd for her arrest, not if it was something to do with Holy Joe. Bishop Todd had nothing to do with some bogeyman from the Dark Ages.

So what did Abby have to do with him, then?

The downpour was unrelenting. Ming's shabby little street was murky with rain, the broken tarmac pock-marked with puddles, the terraced houses miserable and wet-stained. I was shivering and soaked by the time I got to Ming's door, and only when I'd knocked and stood waiting for some time did I realise I'd been stupid. Just because I happened, on the spur of the moment, to need Ming like I needed oxygen, he wasn't guaranteed to be there for me.

Except that he always had been.

The sky was a big dark bruise from horizon to horizon, and there was no sign of the rain letting up. Water dripped down my back and lashed my face. I couldn't get any wetter, so I might as well head on home. Where Griff would be waiting for me, and Dad wouldn't. Where the cops might already have come to interview Mum.

Oh, no way. I felt sick at the thought of going home. Oh please, I begged, ringing the bell one last time. Please, Ming, be here. Teleport yourself from wherever you are and *be in*.

The door whipped open and his pale face peered round it.

'You're soaked.' He dragged me in and slammed the door, then stood staring at me in the cramped hallway. There was hardly room for both of us, and I nearly fell over the brass artillery shell that was stuffed with old walking sticks. Ming shunted it against the wall, out of my way. 'You're soaked. You're mad.'

Almost roughly he shoved me into the tiny lounge his parents insisted on calling a sitting room, then disappeared upstairs. From his armchair Keyser Soze lifted his scarred ginger head and glowered at me, lazily extending five twinkling claws as if daring me to move him. Not there, then.

The massive old sofa took up most of the room, like an uneasy guest, but it was very comfy. Shivering, I sank gratefully into its embrace, trying not to squirm under Keyser Soze's feline glare as I watched the TV news and waited for Ming.

That bloody woman again. Her falcon-eyed spokesman was doing the talking this time. He stood a little in front of Ma Baxter, almost protectively, and he was describing the intense anxiety of the Mother of the Nation for her spiritual guide and close personal friend, Bishop Todd Lamont.

She had spent the morning at prayer for his safe return, along with her entire Cabinet. Fears were growing that the much-loved holy man had been kidnapped and perhaps murdered by fanatics linked to the Schismatic Movement, or even secularist radicals. Feelings were running high among followers of Bishop Todd, indeed among devout One Church members nationwide. The government was extremely concerned that violence might erupt. The Faithful must try to control their understandable emotion, but it would be hardly surprising if…

The camera cut to a montage of demonstrations across the country, demanding Bishop Todd's safe return. Candles lit. Placards waved, not all of their sentiments religiously forgiving. Behind flimsy barriers, a crowd of angry faces screamed insults at the junior Transport Minister, famously sympathetic to schism and now wearing a look of panic on his scrawny face as he plunged through the mob towards his car with the help of his less-than-diligent police escort. One of the cops smiled as a flung missile hit the man on the cheek, and that made me think of what Jeremiah had said about the police.

Ming came back into the room and chucked two bath-towels at me. 'I'm sorry,' he said. 'I thought I heard the bell but I didn't think it could be anyone I wanted to see. I was watching this.'

'Sorry,' I said.

'Don't be.' Standing behind me, he began absently to rub my hair with another towel, and I heard the cat hiss. 'God. Look at that.'

I looked. The mob faces were filled with manic hate, half of them unable to keep the grinning glee off their faces. Their eyes fairly shone with the thrill of righteous grief. One of them was very recognisable, probably because that twisted expression was his natural one. He stood at the very front of the crowd, shoving against a barrier, and brandished a placard that said *Death for Godless Murdrers. Justise for Bishop Todd.*

'Jeremiah Maclaren,' said Ming bitterly.

'Yeah. Bishop Todd's biggest fan.'

'They probably bussed in the whole Scripture Corps.' Ming shivered: I felt it even through his fingertips. 'How fanatical would you have to be?'

'That's Jeremiah for you.' I shrugged. 'He never shuts up about Todd, y'know. Always quoting him. He reckons he'll get some important job in Todd's office when he leaves school. Stupid jerk.' I couldn't resist adding, 'He's had it now.'

'You're wrong.' Ming stared dully at the baying mob. 'Jeremiah doesn't need Todd. He'll be an Assembly Member within five years of graduating. Guaranteed. After that the only way is up.'

Yeah, the polar opposite of Ming. I tried to give him a sympathetic look, but he draped the towel over my head and I heard the sighing click of the TV being turned off, then the remote being dropped onto the floor.

In distracted silence, Ming rubbed at my hair. I liked his fingertips massaging my scalp. I liked it very much. I liked the deep echoing tick of the ancient clock that had belonged to Ming's great-grandmother. I liked the smell of dog that still impregnated the sofa, even though they'd lost their dogs when they lost their land. I wasn't mad keen on Keyser Soze, smuggest cat in the world for outlasting all those friendly floppy hounds, but I liked the way this horrible little house felt like a home, just because of the people who lived in it.

'You're soaking,' Ming said again, as if he'd just noticed. *That* line was getting lame.

'I forgot to take a coat.'

'How could you forget? It hasn't stopped raining since you went home.'

'I wasn't thinking.'

His fingers paused in my hair, then pulled off the towel. 'Why? What's wrong?'

'Abby's been arrested,' I said in a small voice.

He stood quite still, twisting the towel in his hands. At last I turned my head to stare up at him. He was very close to crying.

'So have my parents.'

'*Ming*.' Terrible as it sounds, I forgot about Abby on the spot. 'Why?'

Ming nodded at the blank television screen.

'*Todd?*' My stomach clenched. I thought I was going to be sick.

'They're rounding up everybody.' He found his voice. 'Usual suspects. Y'know? Questioning secularists. Trying to scare people.' He sounded choked. 'Managing.'

'We've got to…' I began. I tried again. 'We've got to…' Then I stopped, because I didn't know what we had to do. 'Ming. Oh, hell. Oh, hell.'

'Shut up,' he said. 'Shut up, I don't want to talk about it. I don't want to think about it. Come on, I've got to find you some clothes.' He said again, like a mantra: 'You're soaked.'

I didn't want to stay with the gangster cat so I followed Ming upstairs and sat on the edge of his bed while he moved around the room like an automaton. He rummaged in a drawer till he found a t-shirt and jeans and a big jumper of indeterminate colour. I took the bundle of clothes in my arms, trying to inhale without looking too obvious. The jumper smelt great. It smelt of Ming.

'I'm really sorry,' I said. I really was. I felt like an idiot, dumping myself on him just when he wanted to curl up in a miserable ball and shut out the world.

'No, it's okay.' He knelt beside the bed and ducked his head under it. 'I know I've got a clean pair of socks somewhere. You need socks. Your feet'll get cold.'

'I don't need socks. Forget it.'

'Yeah, you do.' Without even looking he reached out a hand and clasped it round my cold damp left foot. 'Feel that.'

Mm, yeah. Feel *that*.

I told myself I thought he'd be scrabbling under that bed for ages. I told myself he wasn't looking. I told myself I wasn't thinking. But I was, I was thinking just fine when I undid my shirt and slipped it off just as he resurfaced with one sock in his hand.

His eyes opened wide. Half-heartedly I drew the jumper against me, and we stared at each other. Ming clasped his hands behind his neck, then unclasped them. He put his hands over his face, then brought them down again.

He sat back on his hunkers and watched me solemnly. 'I'm sorry about Abby.'

A little embarrassed now, I pulled his t-shirt over my head. 'I'm sorry about your mum and dad.'

It wasn't the first time they'd been arrested, of course. Happened every now and again. You could set your watch by the government crackdowns, and Ming was good at living alone. He could cook and clean and iron for himself, do all kinds of things I wouldn't begin to know about. He'd get doggedly on with life till they came back many days later, thin and worn out, shame-faced and smiling and promising not to get into trouble again. It must have been like looking after a pair of teenagers. But I liked his mum and dad, I really did. So did Ming, for all his rolling eyes and snide remarks. Between the three of them they always made out it was no big deal, that was life, what could you expect, these things happened.

But it felt different this time, it really did. I knew it, and so did Ming.

'The thing is, I'm worried. I'm thinking about them,' he said. 'All the time.'

'Yeah. Course you are.' I tugged off my jeans, and pulled on his dry ones instead. Hopeless. They floated round my scrawny hips, but at least I was decent. Retrieving my own belt, I yanked it through the belt loops and cinched Ming's jeans tighter.

'Cause, see, despite Mum and Dad saddling me with the most embarrassing name on the planet, I do actually love them. Y'know?'

'Yeah, I know.' I was kind of fond of them, too. 'And I mean, it could be worse. Your surname could be, um… Sidebottom.'

'Smellie,' he suggested. 'I could be Minger Smellie.'

'Pronounced Smiley.'

We both snorted, and giggled for a while, and then we

fell silent. To fill in time I stuck my arms into his old jumper and dragged it over my head. The sleeves were so long I had to go looking for my hands, but the wool was soft and scratchy and cosy. I didn't want to take it off, ever again. Except under *very* specific circumstances.

'Look, Cass.' Ming wriggled uneasily. 'It's just that...'

'What?'

He raked his hands through his hair. 'If I kiss you or something,' he barked, 'doesn't mean I'm not thinking about them. Doesn't mean I've forgotten them. See?'

'Of course.' My heart crashed in my chest.

'Cass,' he moaned. 'Will you stay for a bit?'

'Uh-huh,' I said.

He pulled aside the duvet and flopped back. I thought for a moment about being reticent and modest, and preserving my pride. And then I thought about Aunt Abby, lonely and cold in a police cell with only her dignity for company, and I lay back beside him. Ming put his arm round me, pulled me against him, and with his other arm flicked the duvet back over us both.

I snuggled against him, belatedly cold from my soaking. His body was warm and familiar and I could feel the thud of his heartbeat through his ribs. I could feel the thud of my own, too. But we were both fully clothed, except that I'd never got around to putting on that wretched stupid sock. It wasn't like anything could happen.

His body heat seeped into me till I stopped shivering. I felt completely relaxed, but not sleepy. Not sleepy at all. I splayed my fingers across his chest and stared at them, curling and straightening against him almost of their own volition. He was thin but as strong and taut as a length of rope, and wound just as tight. I watched my fingers flex and curl against him, felt him tense even more.

'Cass…'

'M-hm.'

He laid his hand over mine, interlinking our fingers. 'Stop doing tha…' he began, then hesitated.

The threatened kiss was not forthcoming, and never would be at this rate. Time to take a bit of initiative. I pulled myself half on top of him, touched his lips with my fingertips – I don't know why, to test for resistance or something – and kissed him. For a moment he didn't react, then he threaded his hands into what there was of my hair and kissed me back.

My left leg was hooked over his and I could feel his hips kind of arching up towards me. That made me kiss him more fiercely. He made a helpless sound in his throat, seized my shoulders and turned me onto my back. He did that quite gently, and when he put his trembling hand between my legs that was done gently too. He wasn't the least bit rough when he rolled over and lay on top of me. And I did love him to distraction.

So God alone knew why I kicked him in the nuts.

I didn't mean to, it wasn't a conscious thing. Panic looped round my throat like a garrotte, that was all, and I jerked my knee up before I knew what I was doing. I don't think I got him too hard, since I was at a bad angle for it and the duvet was tangling my legs, but he was so shocked I didn't even have to shove him off. He tumbled off me but when he reached for me I backhanded his fingers so hard he yelled and clutched them with his other hand. He looked at me with pain and disbelief in his eyes.

No. Not disbelief. *Guilt*.

It was his hands on me, you see. It was his hands I couldn't bear, his fat grub hands, and his sweaty grunting weight, and his sticky grinning breath, and – *no!* No, Ming didn't have grub hands, Ming's body wasn't fat and sweaty, *no no no no no* and the voices were loud and clear in my head, screaming at me, and –

I was gasping for breath, but that was just the remnants of animal terror. The back of my hand hurt where I'd hit him, but I'd hurt him more. I could tell by the way he had both his hands between his legs and his lip caught between his teeth, not to mention the tears stinging his eyes.

I reached up to grab handfuls of my hair, pull and wrench it, but there wasn't any there. There just wasn't enough hair to grab –

– and there was a reason for that –

– and I say God alone knew why I'd kicked Ming, but that wasn't true, not any more. Not God alone. Me too. I knew. I *knew*.

Todd's hands, Todd's breath, Todd's slug body –

Somebody had snapped the ringpull, the pressure in my skull had burst, and you know how it is when the contents are erupting out of the can like Krakatoa and you can't stop them going everywhere? That's how it was. I didn't say anything, couldn't make a sound. There was no hair to wrench but I put my hands on my head like I was trying to stop the fizz coming out – I think I can be excused a weird reaction here – and then I got free of the duvet and staggered up, turned and ran.

I could hear Ming pounding down the stairs behind me, yelling my name, but I was way ahead of him. I heard another sound coming from the opposite direction but I didn't recognise it, didn't even register it until I'd flung the front door open and saw Griff's hand poised halfway to hammering on it again. He managed to stop his fist in mid-air – just – and I caught one glimpse of his shocked face before I shoved him aside and pelted out into the rain, barefoot, straight between two parked cars and into the road.

Did it happen like this the first time? Probably something very similar, except that this time the driver had better reactions. That was better luck than I deserved, especially in this weather. The scream of brakes finally cut through the jumbled wasteland of my brain but instead of flinging myself out of the way I just turned on my heel and stared at the car bonnet as it jolted to a halt against my thighs, the wheels sending up great curving fans of rainwater. Streams of water ran off the paintwork, which was a pale metallic green: a very calming, restful colour. I didn't want to look up at the driver but I did, meeting his eyes almost sheepishly through the steady to-and-fro beat of the windscreen wipers. His mouth was open, sagging horribly, and his skin looked drained and taut, his knuckles white on the steering wheel. Amazing how much information the surface of your brain can register in a single instant, even while it's trying to process all those files you lost earlier.

Then I sat down in the sodden road, right in front of him.

I'm sure that driver was a nice responsible guy and I'm sure he'd have stayed to see I was all right. In fact he started to take off his seatbelt, but he never got any further. Griff wrenched his door open and shouted, 'Piss off! Go on, beat it! She's okay! Just *piss off!'*

The poor man, I remember thinking. What had he ever done? He tried to protest, but Griff screamed right in his face this time. 'Her father's clergy! One Church! Now get out of here, okay? Beat it!' He slammed the door again and kicked it for good measure, and this time, the panicking driver started his stalled engine with a horrible noise and the car reversed down the street through pools of water. He did a seven-point turn in a clumsy squeal of tyres and got out of there as fast as he could.

Ming was on his knees beside me in the drenching, deafening rain but Griff grabbed him by his collar and hauled him to his feet. I thought for a moment he was going to kill him but I couldn't do anything. My brain was still filing, still defragmenting, and I couldn't move.

Griff was swearing incoherently at Ming, but Ming didn't even react. His face was drained of blood, rain sluicing down it and dripping off his chin.

'What have you done?' yelled Griff, his words suddenly comprehensible – and repeatable – once more. *'What have you done?* I told you this would happen, you stupid, stupid – '

'Leave him alone,' I managed to say, but I could hardly hear my own voice against the batter of rain on parked cars. 'Leave him alone.'

Clasping my hands behind my neck, I watched as Ming shook Griff off and stood there trembling. There was a huge gaping void around me where there was no noise and no wind, like being in an invisible pod, protected by a forcefield of lies. I couldn't even feel the rain that lashed me. The only sound I could hear was my own voice, and I was amazed how clear and calm and level it was.

'It wasn't you.' I smiled at Griff. 'It wasn't you at all. Was it? It was me. Bishop Todd raped me.'

13: What Todd Did Next

Now here's how I felt.

You know that film *Demon*, the one with all the sequels: *Demon II* and *Demon Invasion* and *Demon Resurrection* and so on? And you know that terrible moment in the first film, when the very first demon comes out of the space missionary's ribcage? It's been living in there unsuspected, ever since he got attacked by the thing in the egg, and he's happily living his life and eating his breakfast or whatever and it just bursts out.

Well, that's how I felt, only my demon couldn't get out. Okay, I knew it was there now, and it was digging and biting and scrabbling inside me but damn, my bones and my flesh were too strong. It couldn't make a dent. And I wished it would, I wished it would just explode out of my chest so I could die and stop it biting.

But meanwhile I smiled at a spot in the middle distance. I don't know what else they expected me to do, and if I stopped smiling long enough to think, I was just going to die anyway.

Me and my demon.

• • •

We sat there in the rain, all three of us on the kerb, Ming and Griff on either side of me. Griff's arms rested on his knees and he was staring across the road. Ming had his head in his hands and he wasn't saying a word. I watched the brown filthy rain as it gurgled and swirled down the iron drain cover at my bare feet. We were all soaked and the rain was still falling, relentless. We were alone, nobody was around. Nobody sane would be.

'It didn't go quite that far.' Griff didn't look at me. He didn't want to say the word, the word for how far it apparently didn't go. 'He really hurt you. I mean, he was about to – but I walked in as he was…' He took a breath. 'If he'd actually – Dad would have killed him.'

'Would he?' I paddled my toes in the rainwater.

'I nearly did.'

'You're not Dad,' I said.

To avoid Griff's troubled glance I studied Ming's hands against his face. The fingers raked into his hair were long and thin, with prominent knuckles. Not like the Bishop's. Not like those fat white grubs. All the same I wondered if I'd ever in my life be able to contemplate them touching me, ever again.

'It went far enough,' I said.

Griff was silent for so long that I turned and looked at him. In the driving rain I couldn't decide if he was crying. 'I'm sorry. I'm so sorry. Thing is, I left. I'd served at the altar that day. Dad was preaching somewhere else and Todd was the guest preacher at our church, and afterwards I was kind of torn between staying and talking to him, or rushing home to see *The Exorcism Files*. You know how much I liked Todd but he seemed kind of brusque that day. It was almost like he wanted rid of me. If I'd stopped to think about it I might have wondered.'

'No you wouldn't,' I said. 'Why should you?'

Griff didn't answer that. 'He told me to go ahead, said he was waiting for Dad, so you could stay and wait with him. He'd been kind of joking around with you all morning, and I was jealous he was paying you so much attention. I didn't even get suspicious, you know. I wouldn't have come back at all if I hadn't forgotten my jacket and my keys hadn't been in the pocket. But I should have guessed. I should have known.' Griff was definitely crying now, but his voice stayed steady. 'I should never have left you.'

I didn't feel like crying. I felt perfectly calm, despite that demon in my ribcage. 'How, precisely? You were thirteen. How would you have known?'

He sniffed and rubbed the back of his arm across his face. 'I couldn't believe what I was seeing. When I went in the vestry, I mean. You're not big now but you were so small. You'd just turned eleven. Eleven, for God's sake. I grabbed that wonky candlestick, the one that was coming off its base, the one that needed soldering. I couldn't think what else to do.'

'Of course you couldn't.'

'No. Yes. Actually, I wasn't thinking anything at all. He had a hold of you by the hair, he had a great big fistful of your hair, Cass, and I just wanted to make him let go. I swung the thing at him, as hard as I could. I missed, but he had to let you go. You ran. You just ran, you didn't scream or anything, and I should have followed you, but I was too angry and I was frightened.' He swallowed hard. 'Do you remember it all?'

'No,' I said. 'Bits. Vague bits. I keep remembering more.' I didn't want to.

He was silent again for ages, while the rain ran off us,

soaking us to the skin. I could feel it trickling between my toes, dripping down my neck and my back, running off my eyelashes and getting in my eyes. My brain knew it was fresh colourless rainwater but I imagined it was just like the grimy water in the gutter, thick and brown and scummy. It was soaking through my skin, staining my innards, and I'd never get it off. Not in a million years.

'You never screamed,' said Griffin.

I don't know if that was an accusation or what. I didn't really care. 'I was scared of him,' I said, remembering. 'I was so scared. He was scary.' Mystified, I shook my head. 'He always seemed so…'

'Nice,' said Griff.

'Funny,' I said. 'Cuddly.'

'I broke the candlestick against the wall. I swung it so hard I could have killed him, and maybe I meant to. I was aiming for his head and he knew it. So he grabbed the bits of candlestick and he threw them through that window. That stained glass window. Dad really liked it.'

'Yes.' I stared at the swirl of filthy rain in the gutter.

'He grabbed me. He got me by the throat, I thought he'd kill me. Cass. I don't think he'd have let go if Dad hadn't come in. He came in the back door of his own church and found an Arch-Rector with his hands round his son's throat.' He shut his eyes. 'I never felt so helpless or useless or angry. Then we heard the screams outside, and the car hitting the wall after it hit…' His voice died.

'*You* weren't useless,' I told him calmly.

'Yeah. I was so busy being a superhero I let you run under that car.'

'So did Dad.'

'Don't blame Dad,' said Griff miserably. 'You should have heard the things they said to each other later. God.'

'Yes, I bet they had a bit of a squabble.'

'Please, Cass. Please.'

I sighed. 'Didn't somebody notice at the hospital? I mean, did somebody ask why I ran under a car?'

'Far as the staff knew you'd just been fooling around, you'd run into the road without looking. I think there was a nurse who saw more, and a doctor. The doctor, he got posted to the islands where the army were fighting rebels, and he hasn't been heard of since. The nurse just disappeared. Y'know?' He couldn't help adding bitterly, 'The way they do.'

Lovely. Blood on my hands, on top of everything else.

'Mum and Dad didn't know anything either, not then, they didn't ask questions. All they cared about was you not dying. But when you were sort of stable, Dad took me home. His head was in pieces, he was so confused, and that's when he asked me what had happened. Why was I fighting with Todd, for God's sake? When I told him, he had to park the car for about twenty minutes. His hands wouldn't stop shaking, he was so angry I was scared for him.

'And when we got home? Todd was right there in our house. Cocky as hell. He must have taken the keys from my jacket pocket, cool as that. Dad went for him, threatened to kill him, but he couldn't follow through. Not Dad. And I think he really wanted to hear Todd explain himself, he was desperate to hear an apology, some kind of remorse.'

'An apology,' I said coldly.

'What if Dad had killed him?' For the first time Griff sounded as if he could get angry with me. 'What do you think would have happened to him? You only had to hear Todd when he got his breath back. The things he said. Oh, Cass. The things he threatened Dad with. He was going to have you and me taken away. He said he'd blame Dad for everything and I mean *everything*. Do you understand what I'm saying? He'd say *Dad abused you*. Imagine it, Cass.'

'No,' I said. My hands had started to shake too.

'He said no-one would believe Dad. That's true. Todd could have accused him of anything. Nobody would take your word or mine, Cass. We were kids, he was our father. Todd was going to say *he'd* intervened, that he'd walked in on Dad…The police would have sided with Todd, even if they had to fabricate evidence. Do you see? Dad had no choice. None.'

'None,' I echoed.

But he had. He'd had another choice, one day in the woods, and he'd taken it because it was better than the last choice, anything would be. Because it was the first choice he'd been given in the matter, and he'd taken it.

I still couldn't forgive him. Or her. 'Mum knew,' I said.

'Uh-huh. Of course.'

'And you knew. And…' I glanced aside at Ming, my best friend, my oldest friend, the love of my life.

'Sometimes we thought you knew. That you'd remembered.' Griff smiled weakly. 'Like when you cut all your hair off. We thought you'd remembered then, but you hadn't.'

'No. I remember doing that but I didn't know why. Because that's how he kept hold of me, that's why I did it.'

Griff looked at the sky, letting rain sting his eyes. 'Dad said to him, *You call yourself a man of God!* And Todd gave him that dimply smirk, that one he had when he was really pleased with himself. Y'know? And he said, *But, Gabriel, it's what I call myself that matters!*'

'He's right.' Suddenly I felt exhausted. 'I want to go home now.'

Not that I knew what I'd do when I got there, or whether I'd even stay. A part of me just wanted somebody to come along and take pity on me and hit me with a stick like they should have done before. That was only a small part, though. The rest of me wanted to take a stick myself, and kill my parents.

14: Running

Nothing was going my way. It's not possible to keep rage boiling away forever without running out of energy, and I had to sit curled in an armchair and hugging my knees for hours. Mum had been taken down to the police station to give a statement about some other bloody mystery I'd never been told about, and Dad was still there, never having come home in the first place.

I watched the relentless rain make patterns on the windows. I bit my nails methodically down to the quick, one at a time. I tried to watch television, but there was nothing but bad soaps and gameshows and endless news bulletins, and if I saw Ma Baxter's mournful brave face once more I'd throw something through the screen. And I didn't want to waste any more rage. It was burning down to a single bright ember inside me and I had to nurse it, like I nursed my demon, keeping it happy in there so it wouldn't kill me.

Griff didn't want to leave me on my own but I made him go. I thought he'd go upstairs and lose himself in *Hell Breaker II* but he didn't. He put on Dad's long black raincoat and went outside and stood in the rain. God knew how he kept his cigarettes alight but now and again I'd see weak little trails of wet smoke drift across the window. I hadn't made him stand outside, so I didn't feel guilty. I didn't feel angry with him. I didn't blame him like I blamed them. I kept hearing Mum say *He's never got over it you know*, and the soft spot I had for my brother was getting softer by the minute.

Those nights were long and light, but it was nearly dark by the time the parents slouched home. I heard the gravel crunch wetly, the rain settle to a dull drumming on the car roof, the engine killed into silence, the creak and slam of the doors. Griff must have intercepted them, because they took a few seconds too long to come into the house, and when they did they just stared at me, red-eyed, Dad as pale as death and Mum twisting her hands together as if she was trying to unscrew them.

I wasn't crying. If either of them did, I thought I might slap them, but they didn't.

Well, I wanted to say, what did the pair of you think? That I'd never remember? Did you think I'd go through life with this locked inside me? Did you think the demon was going to like it so much in there it would curl up in my chest and go to sleep and never want to see the outside world?

I never said any of that, of course. I kept my mouth shut, because if I opened it the demon might get out that way.

'We didn't know how much you remembered,' Mum said at last. 'We never knew.'

'You never tried to find out.' My voice sounded like somebody else's. Maybe it was.

'I was scared to.' She put the side of her hand into her mouth and bit it.

'We didn't want to remind you,' said Dad. 'Different if he'd been punished.'

'He was,' I said. Was that my demon's voice? Certainly wasn't mine.

Dad took a silent breath. 'Not then.'

'But now,' I said. 'Now he's been punished.'

Mum sat down very abruptly on the sofa. Her teeth dug so hard into the skin of her hand I thought she'd draw blood. I was interested to see if she would, so I watched it closely.

'Do you understand we couldn't do anything?' said Dad. His voice sounded alien too.

'Yes,' I told him.

'But you don't forgive us.'

'No.' I sighed deeply, while the demon punched my rib-cage. *Down, boy*, I told it. See, I was getting used to it already. 'Know what? I could forgive you when I thought it was Griff. I understood. I was okay about it when my *brother* got assaulted. There was nothing you could do. It was awful but it couldn't be helped, it wasn't your fault.' I took a breath. 'And now I know it was me? I'm not okay about it. At all. It's not a terrible necessity and I don't understand it, because it was *me*.' I gave Dad a cold little smile. 'Can you see why I feel lower than a slug?'

Strands of black hair had fallen across Dad's eyes. They'd been wet with rain but by this time they'd dried and stiffened to spikes. He didn't push them away; he was trying to hide behind them, but it was no good. His eyes were hardly blue at all, they were dilated and indigo.

'We're sorry, Cass,' he said. 'We're so sorry.'

Sure they were. 'How's Abby?' I asked.

'Um.' Dad rubbed his hand across his face, several times. 'She's... fine. Fine.'

Well, that was another lie. Oh, so what.

'I don't want to know about it,' I told him. 'I don't want

to know why she's there. I don't want to know another secret just now.'

'All right.'

'I'm going to go now.'

They were silent for ages. 'Go,' echoed Dad at last. 'Where to?'

I stood up. 'Well, I'll have to go to Ming's,' I said. 'I can't think of anywhere else. I'll be all right there. You'll know where I am.'

'Will Mrs Urquhart…' began Mum. She faltered. 'Will she be okay with that?'

'Of course she will,' I said frostily. 'She's like me. She doesn't ask awkward questions.'

'No.' Mum bit her lip.

'I mean, they live in a slum and everything,' I said sarcastically, 'but there's always room on their sitting room floor. They're very welcoming. They're nice people.'

'Perhaps I should…' Mum's voice petered out. 'Yes. All right.'

I could have thrown it in their faces that Mrs Urquhart wouldn't be there and neither would her husband, but I held my tongue. If I told them, they might still try to stop me going. I resented not being angry enough to tell them and defy them anyway.

'I'll call her,' said Mum dully. 'Let her know you're coming. That's only… polite.' She half-swallowed the last word, knowing fine how it would clang in my brain in the circumstances.

I went upstairs to pack.

Neither of them tried to follow me and talk me out of it, and I didn't know whether to be sad or relieved about that.

When I came downstairs, dragging my backpack and my sleeping bag, they were in exactly the same position, as if they hadn't moved or breathed or spoken a word since I'd left the room. You know that moment when you realise that not only are your parents not omnipotent, they're utterly helpless in the face of the world? Well, that was it for me.

I tucked my sleeping bag awkwardly under my arm. It was a big padded lie, that sleeping bag, since I had no intention of using it. I didn't care. Deviousness was in my genes.

'It was on answerphone,' said Mum. Her mobile phone hung in her limp hand. 'I left a message. I hope that's okay.'

She knew it was okay, it was always okay. Mum never spoke to Ming's mum or dad if she could help it; she didn't want cosy chats with troublemakers. If my parents and Ming's parents had an answerphone relationship, it was of Mum's making. Right now, I was having no trouble keeping my balance here on the moral high ground.

'Give me a call if there's a problem, *any* problem,' said Mum. Then she took a breath and made a massive adjustment. 'Ask Mrs Urquhart to call me if you don't want to talk to me.'

'Yeah,' I said. 'Okay.'

'I'll drive you,' said Dad.

I took a breath to say no, but what came out was 'All right.'

• • •

I had to say goodbye to Griff. He was in the garden, under a dripping rowan, gazing down at the twilit valley. You could hear the low roar of the river even above the lashing rain. The dusk obscured its violent torrent but you could make out that the trees on its banks were still clear of the water.

'Have you seen it?' said Griff. 'Have you seen the river?'

I went to stand beside him.

'You're going, then. Thought you would.' He looked down at the gorge.

'Don't be angry with me,' I said.

'Course I'm not angry with you.'

'Only I'm going to Ming's. Just for a bit,' I added.

'Fine. I like him, don't I? Go ahead, be happy *for a bit*.' He smiled at me without showing his teeth, one of his tight little real smiles. 'What difference does it make now?'

'Bye,' I told him. 'See you later.'

• • •

Dad didn't say a word, all the way to Ming's, just rubbed his hand across his face now and again. It was almost dark now so I couldn't see the colour of his eyes, but he kept pushing his hair out of them and his fingers were trembling. My handsome fallen-angel Dad. My lovely murderer. My avenger. I still loved him but I needed to try and hate him for a while.

'Are they in?' he asked doubtfully as the car skidded in the puddled rainwater outside Ming's door.

'You can wait if you like,' I bluffed. 'Check.'

I shut the car door and hitched my backpack onto one shoulder, then lifted my sleeping bag. No light showed through the thick overlong curtains that belonged in a much bigger house, but a rectangle of dim light opened as Ming came to the door, silent and blinking. His left eye was half-closed, bruised and cut quite badly, and his lip was split. I couldn't believe he'd managed to get in a fight in the short time I'd been away but I wasn't in any position to give him a hard time about it.

'Hello,' I said.

'Hello.'

'Can I stay?' I put all my desperation into the look I gave him, hoping we were still telepathic.

Ming looked past me to Dad's car. 'Hi, Rector Gabriel.'

'Hi, Ming,' Dad called. 'Is your Mum there?'

'She went down to the shop. She'll be back in ten minutes. Dad's in the bath, you want a word?'

Bless you, Ming.

'No, no. It's okay. Is this all right? Did your parents get the phone message?'

'Yeah. S'fine.'

There was silence for a dragging moment, and Dad's uncertainty was almost tangible. Then the engine coughed into life, and as Ming stood back to let me past into the hall, the car pulled away. Hesitating, I turned and watched till it had turned the corner. There was no way I could really see Dad's blue eyes in the rearview mirror. But I imagined I did, and I was still seeing them as I walked into Ming's sitting room and heard the front door close quietly behind me.

15: Taking Precautions

It was still raining. I could hear the desultory dash of it against the windows and the roof, occasionally rising to a thunderous clatter before it faded again, but it never stopped, not altogether. I wished it would.

An unpromising dawn filtered through Ming's curtains, greying his bedroom with dull light though it was barely four o'clock. There wasn't much night at this time of year.

Funny, but I hadn't been scared at all. No wild reactions, no involuntary shudders, no flinching, no kicking him in the nuts. Far from it, actually. It was fine. Better than fine.

What I liked just as much, though, was lying here with Ming's arm round me, his face turned towards mine in his sleep, his breath against my forehead, his hair tickling my cheek. I liked having so much of my skin touching so much of his. I liked my legs being tangled up in his, and my hand splayed against his chest to feel the rise and fall of his ribcage and the slow drowsy thump of his heart.

I even liked the hot and bothered feeling of being so close to him and remembering what we'd got up to and not being able to do it again because he was asleep. It was a pleasant tingling sort of frustration. My fingers tightened against his chest, and as if responding he rolled onto his side in his sleep. I drew back a tiny distance to focus on his sleeping face. His mouth creased up at the corners, and his eyelids twitched in a dream. His left eye was in quite a state, and I suspected that even when he woke up it was not going to open. There was still a little bruising and yellowness on the edge of his right eye socket, too, from his last run-in with Jeremiah's gang. His upper lip was swollen with the new cut, and an old scar about a centimetre long ran up from it. There were speckles of dried blood just inside his nostrils, and a slight bump on his nose where it had once been broken. Ming's face had quite a history for its age. It really was beautiful. It wasn't a perfect face but I loved it.

Lying there it crossed my mind to be glad I'd fallen out with Mum and Dad, and to hope Ming's parents wouldn't be released just yet. Not tonight...

As if I didn't feel enough of a slug already, now I felt like something on the heel of Ming's shoe. But it wasn't my fault they'd been arrested. Not entirely and directly my fault. Nor was my quarrel with Mum and Dad my fault, unless I'd engineered my unwillingness to be in the same house. Which I might have, a tiny bit. But I was truly hurt, and confused, and angry, and maybe I wanted to hurt, confuse and anger them right back.

I wriggled carefully around so that my back was to Ming. He stirred but didn't wake, and his body nestled more comfortably against mine, his arms tightening around me. We fitted perfectly together, like we'd been made that way.

I must have slept, because when I was next aware of anything our positions were reversed. Ming lay with his back to me and I was curled against him, one arm hooked around him, my cheek pressed between his shoulder blades. I knew he was awake, though: I could tell from the tension in his body.

My horrible dream frayed and dissipated, lost in the reality of Ming's presence, and I was grateful. I could remember only a little, and that was more than enough. I'd been slamming my fist hard into someone's head, someone whose face I couldn't see. I was striking them so hard the skull crumpled, not like paper exactly but as easily as squashing an empty Coke can. There was a lot of blood but I was surprised how cold it felt where it drenched my fingers. Now that I was awake, I tried to move my right hand, but it was numb where I lay on it.

The remote control was in Ming's hand and the little television under the window was on, the volume turned very low. I couldn't see the screen but I could hear the cheery morning signature tune of the Breakfast News. I could picture Tanya Moonfleet's psychotic morning smile, could hear her giggling and flirting with her co-presenter and then turning so serious so quickly you'd think she was bipolar. Dad and I used to watch her over breakfast, open-mouthed, plotting her horrible death over the toast rack.

That didn't seem quite such a joke any more.

'The Commissioner of Police has released details of a man wanted for questioning about the presumed kidnapping of Bishop Todd Lamont.' Her voice thick with concern. Tanya paused, presumably while a picture flashed onto the screen. 'Colum Quinn, disgraced former editor of the *Questioner*, has not been seen since late last week when his newspaper's offices were raided by police and closed down on charges of sedition, blasphemy and libel. While fears continue to grow for Bishop Todd's safety, police are anxious to talk to Mr Quinn, but fear that he has already crossed the border in an attempt to evade justice.'

They switched to an outside broadcast; you could hear the change in sound quality, the muted roar of traffic and the patter of rain on umbrellas. I recognised the voice of the Security minister. 'We are confident that extradition will be swift despite the absence of any formal treaty with our neighbours. Harbouring an enemy of our state would after all constitute an act of aggression that we and our allies could not tolerate, and we demand Mr Quinn's immediate and unconditional rendition...'

'That's that journalist,' I mumbled. 'Quinn.'

Ming clicked off the television and looked over his shoulder. 'Hi,' he said, and smiled.

'Hi,' I said back. There was a spot between his shoulder blades that needed kissing, so I obliged. I felt him squirm and was pleased with myself.

Ming reached out to lay the remote on the bedside table. 'I'll turn round in a minute,' he muttered. 'But could you do that again?'

Well, I aimed to please.

After a bit he wriggled round and kissed me. 'I love you,' he said.

My heart floated. 'Yeah. Likewise. That's that journalist they were talking about,' I said again. 'The one that interrupted Ma Baxter's press conference.'

'Uh-huh.' Ming let his forefinger trace my hairline. 'Listen, about Todd, and... and you. I'm sorry, Cass.'

'It's not your fault,' I told him coolly. 'They wouldn't let you tell me, right?'

'No.' He chewed the corner of his mouth, the tip of his tongue running across his new scar, and slewed his eyes away from mine. 'Griff didn't like me touching you. In case I…'

'Quite,' I said. 'I know.'

'Well, he was right.'

'Might have happened anyway,' I pointed out. 'And I had to remember sometime.'

'Did you?'

'Yeah.'

'That's… well, that's kind of what I thought too.'

The funniest thing was, my demon had curled up and died, some time in the night. I could still feel the weight where it had lain, but like an amputated limb, it was only the memory of something that wasn't there any more. My body must have absorbed it, like a splinter you couldn't get out. I'm sure I still had a lot of yelling and sulking and blaming to do, but I wasn't going to die of it. Nobody was. Except one, and I guess he'd done that already. It was nobody's fault, after all. Nobody's but Todd's.

The door creaked open, and a second or two later a warm weight landed on us. Keyser Soze trod a few circles on our bellies, his claws unretracted, then curled up between us, his weight shoving us apart. As Ming rubbed between his scabby ears with a forefinger, the brute began to purr like a train. He pretended to be out of it within seconds, but I wasn't born yesterday. He wasn't asleep, he was jealous.

'You do know your cat's gay,' I told Ming.

He gave a snort of laughter. 'He could have you killed for that.'

'I bet.' I snuggled as close to Ming as I could get, dislodging Keyser Soze. Ten needles sank into my thigh, despite his pretence at unconsciousness, but I ignored the brute.

'Cass,' whispered Ming.

'Mm.'

He took a breath, as if he was gathering up his courage. 'I have to leave. I can't stay in this country, I can't.'

I'd been expecting it, but I felt myself start to cry anyway.

'I might as well go. I won't get back into school now. Your dad's pal Wilf barely got you off the hook, Cass. There's no way he could get me off too.'

I knew that. I felt horribly guilty but what could I do? 'What about your mum and dad?'

'They'll understand. Actually they'll approve. If they ever hear about it.'

My blood froze. 'Meaning what?'

'I've heard. They're not. Coming out this time.' He was gasping for breath in his effort not to cry.

I took his face between my hands and stroked his hair off it. I was afraid to hug him because he was tensed like a cat and I was afraid he'd spring away and run. 'Who told you that? Ming! Who told you that?'

His face was locked into a tight scowl, which was how he'd always suppressed his tears. 'Somebody came last night.'

'A friend?'

He shook his head and swallowed hard. I wanted to wrap him up and stow him away in my ribcage in the space my demon had left. Keep him safe till they'd gone.

'No,' he said at last. 'Somebody who'd seen Mum and

Dad recently. I don't know if he was militia or police, maybe both. He said they'd come for me eventually.'

'Oh, God, Ming. Couldn't you... isn't there someone we could call?'

'Ghostbusters?' His smile failed. 'This guy said, don't bother calling the police, 'cause I'd be wasting my time and theirs. Well, I knew that already.' He rubbed his bruised nose with a fist, and winced. 'He said they couldn't be bothered taking me into care. The state doesn't waste its money on the likes of me. He said I'd better go on taking care of myself 'cause when I'm old enough to hang they'll come and get me for something.'

Oh, God, oh God. 'Cause of Rose?' I whispered.

'No, no. For lots of things. Just for being their son, I think. It's not your fault, Cass, honest. They know fine I didn't do anything to Rose. Wilf saw everything and he's an important guy.'

'So meanwhile they're taking it out on your mum and dad.'

'Cass.' He smiled weakly. 'They take everything out on Mum and Dad. Forget it.'

Slug, slug. I was a slug. It wasn't just that it was all my fault. While I was having my little family crisis and plotting how to run to him and beg for sympathy, Ming was being intimidated by the religious police. Being *beaten up* by them. I was on the brink of self-hatred but since that would be just another version of feeling sorry for myself, I stopped my train of thought in its tracks, and hugged him fiercely.

'I need to go over the border,' he mumbled into my neck. 'Claim asylum. I'm tired, Cass. I'm so tired of getting the crap beaten out of me and I'm not seventeen yet.'

I swallowed my tears and clenched my teeth. 'But it'll be awful. They'll intern you, if they don't send you straight back.'

'I don't care. I've got to try.'

'I'll come with you.'

His arm tightened around me and he kissed my scalp. 'Don't be daft. You've got your family.'

There was nothing I could reasonably say to that, so I kept my mouth shut.

Being with Ming, eating breakfast and washing up and watching television, felt like being wrapped in a warm cocoon, but I could go home and be with my parents any time I wanted. Ming was stuck with his freedom. All the same, I have to admit I was happy. I could even think about Todd and the years of being somebody who wasn't real, and I could still be happy. I'd been a pretend person for so long, maybe it was easy to go on pretending. I was only playing house, playing at real life. But this felt more real than my last four years.

Maybe my brother had more sense of reality than I did. He certainly had more sense, as I remembered when he rang the doorbell later that morning and Ming opened the door as if he was expecting a fist in the face.

Griff only smiled thinly, and held out his hand. 'I won't stay.'

'Sure?' Ming took his hand with some trepidation.

Peering over Ming's shoulder, I smiled at my brother. Actually I nearly laughed. I didn't think Griff was the shaking-the-hand-of-your-sister's-seducer type. Unless he was about to challenge Ming to a duel or something.

As Ming drew his hand away he closed it into a fist. 'Where did you get those?' His eyes were wide. 'They're prescription-only. You need a letter of permission from your rector.'

'I've got sources. And no, I didn't ask Dad.'

I put my hand over my mouth. Ming shoved what Griff had given him into his pocket.

'Oops,' said Griff sarcastically. 'Forget something, Cass?' His eyes strayed back to Ming. 'I suppose you've already been stupid but don't be any stupider, will you?'

'Okay,' said Ming, rubbing his forehead with the back of his hand, wincing as he absently touched his eye.

'What happened to you?' said Griff.

'Just the usual,' said Ming, shrugging.

'Well, watch yourselves. Be careful.' Griff eyed us both. 'In all sorts of ways.'

I pushed past Ming and hugged Griff. He looked a bit surprised but he hugged me back.

'Mum's going to phone you later,' he told me. 'Pretend his parents are in, won't you?'

• • •

Mum called when Ming was out. He'd gone out just before lunchtime, having given me a verbal Rough Guide to Ming's Fridge and the cooker instructions, but all I wanted was some toast. Actually, all I wanted was to go with him, but he wouldn't let me. He'd been so bossy and alpha-male about it I was pissed off with his attitude. And my toast was starting to burn and I couldn't find the cancel button, so when the phone rang I grabbed it and snapped my name into it without thinking.

A hesitant silence. 'Cass.'

'Yeah.' I set my teeth, annoyed at myself. 'Hi, Mum.' Getting my brains back in line, I splayed my fingers over the mouthpiece and shouted, 'Yeah, Mrs Urquhart. S'okay. It's for me.'

Silence again. Suspicious silence. 'Are you all right, Cassandra? Is there anything you need?'

Is there anything I need? What did she think I was going to say? A new brain. A new past. No, Mum, thanks, we're okay for condoms.

'I suppose that was a stupid question,' she said into the silence.

'No, Mum. No. I'm fine, honest.' Rubbing a tear from the corner of my eye, I bit my upper lip. 'I need some time, that's all.' *Oh, and I need to sleep with my boyfriend to remind myself I'm a person, I need to be with him more than I need to be with you, and I love him so much I'm prepared to lie to you and hurt you, and I feel so guilty I think I'll have to shoot myself. Otherwise...* 'I'm fine. How's Aunt Abby?'

'Your father says she's fine. It's... it's a mess, Cassie. It's complicated. I'll explain it to you. I *promise.*'

'All right. It's all right, Mum, really.' And it really was. I had my secrets and they had theirs. That was how the world worked. We couldn't know everything, could we? We'd go mad.

'Can I speak to Mrs Urquhart?'

Oh, don't strain yourself, Mum.

I said, 'She's just gone into the loo. Want me to get her to call you back?' My, I was getting good at the family business of lying.

'It's okay. I'll… I'll call again later.' She hesitated. 'Come home any time, Cass. You know we love you, don't you?'

'Yeah.' I mumbled, 'I love you too.'

'Good.'

When we'd hung up I cried for a bit, and threw my burnt toast in the bin. After that I found it hard to kill the time. I watched *Angels and Martyrs*. They found the body under the patio. Major drama, major hysterics. Myself, I thought they were overreacting.

I fed Keyser Soze, and he bit me on the ankle for my pains. I did some ironing, badly. I watched the news for a bit: more arrests, more demonstrations, a growing diplomatic spat with the neighbours. Wow. It was better soap opera than *Angels and Martyrs*, and Ma Baxter was much the best actress on television.

Nothing about Holy Joe, though. Whatever they'd found they were keeping it quiet. I hoped Abby really was all right. I hoped she wasn't scared, there in her cell. I hoped she wasn't lonely and afraid without the love of her life to cuddle against her and tell her it was all okay, that he was going out but he'd be safe, he'd be back soon, she was safe too and she wasn't to move, please feed the cat and *no she could not go with him*.

And it kept on raining.

Ming came back in the early afternoon, closing the door quietly. He didn't call my name, just came into the kitchen where I sat nursing a lukewarm cup of coffee that was my fifth of the day and was making me nauseous.

Ming spread out his wet newspaper, smoothing it flat, ripping it accidentally but pressing it back together with his fingertips. Carefully he turned the sodden pages.

'Anything?' I asked.

'Nothing.' He lifted another page. 'Nothing about Mum and Dad, of course.' He gave me a rueful glance. 'Nothing about Abby, nothing about Holy Joe. They must be suppressing that, whatever it is. Increasing pressure for that Colum Quinn to be extradited. He's surfaced, apparently. Ma Baxter's getting pretty strident, she'll have us at war if she's not careful.' Shoving his fingers through his wet fringe, he rested his forehead on the heel of his hand. 'Oh, and they're not admitting it, but it looks like they've given up the search for the Bishop.'

'Long ago,' I said. 'He's more use to her missing, isn't he? Diverts everyone from the fact the economy's going down the toilet. That's why the search wasn't very thorough.' I was quite shocked at the bitterness in my voice. Where had that cynical notion come from?

I knew I was right, though.

Shrugging, Ming turned to the back page of the *Messenger*. 'That's it, really. What time does the tide turn?' He peered at the columns, tracing the tables with a finger.

'About five, I think. Why?'

'Five-ten. You're right.' He smiled. Half-standing up, he leaned across the table and kissed me. I touched his ear to try and keep him there but he drew away again, licking his cut lip. 'The cave's underwater.'

I gasped. 'You've been to look?'

'Uh-huh.' He sat down again, placed his hands on the table. 'It's good in a way, Cass. If the cave's full of water it'll wash away... traces. You know.'

Funny, us sitting here discussing this so coolly. If I

stepped back from my body and watched what I was doing, what I was talking about, I wouldn't believe in myself. But I didn't step back, I didn't want a sensible perspective on this. It was best viewed all askew. Otherwise I'd go mad thinking about what we'd done.

I swigged my horrible coffee, made a face and stared at the oily film on its surface. 'And if it washes... *everything* away?'

Ming shrugged again. It was becoming his regular form of expression. 'It might wash right out to sea. Depends on the tide. Even if it gets caught downstream, even if the tide brings it back in, how will there be any evidence on it? Anything they know will be circumstantial.'

Circumstances. Yes, yes.

I watched Ming's face. I thought about his violence, his ruthlessness, his fingers jabbing at Jeremiah's throat and eyes. The scratches and bruising on his face when I found him in the wood, before we found the Bishop, seven lifetimes ago. Spitting on the corpse, and having the gall to go back and clean it off. Going back to the cave just now to check if it was flooded.

Maybe he had to keep going back, maybe it was a compulsion.

And *When you report this leave me out of it*. And *Bishop Todd got the land*.

And I just didn't know any more.

'Did you kill him?' I asked.

I hadn't meant to. I just opened my mouth and out it came. Ming looked at his fingernails and frowned. Then he sighed, and looked up at me.

'No,' he said coolly.

I kept watching his eyes, and swallowed.

'Don't get me wrong,' he said. 'I wish I had. I'd have liked it to be me. But it wasn't.'

'All right,' I said.

Standing up abruptly, Ming switched on the kettle. He pushed down the toaster, empty, then pressed the cancel button. Then he did it again. The sound it made was a clanging mechanical protest, as if he was torturing it.

'You said it was your Dad.' His voice was muffled as he tormented the toaster again.

'Yeah. I know.'

'You said you knew it was him.' Ming sounded alien, bitter and cool. 'And that's why you made me...'

I pulled the crusts off a cold bit of toast I'd made earlier. 'I was so sure. I still think it was, it's just I'm not sure any more. Not absolutely, a hundred-and-ten percent sure. That's all.'

God, I sounded lame. I'd got Ming into possibly the worst trouble of his life because of a suspicion that was only ninety-nine-and-a-bit percent. Methodically I began to shred the stale toast into crumbs, rolling them under my palm. The fragments were hard and sharp enough to hurt, so I rubbed my flesh harder against them. Self-Harm with Toast.

Turning at last, Ming smiled with half his mouth, trying to fake some good humour. 'Don't feel bad about asking.'

But I did. Maybe I'd just wanted to share the blame around. Maybe I'd wanted it to be Ming, because then it wouldn't be Dad. More to the point, it wouldn't be...

'Me,' I blurted, but I had my hands clasped over my mouth and Ming thought I was talking to him.

'What?' he said curtly. He pushed the toaster down again, but this time he didn't press cancel. This time he was going to let it burn the house down. Well, hey. Why not.

'Do you think it was me?' I mumbled.

Moving the flat of his hand over the toaster slots, he let the heat singe his palm. 'Sorry?'

Yanking my hands away, I screamed. '*DO YOU THINK IT WAS ME?*'

Ming's distant half-a-smile died, bitterness creeping into his voice. 'Of course I don't. Cass, I wouldn't think that about *you*.'

'That's not what I mean! I'm not asking for your good opinion!' I started to cry. 'Ming. Do you think it might have been me? Did I kill the Bishop?'

16: Crumbling

You plant a seed in someone's head like that, and it's going to take root. I knew that now, I knew it as Ming's eyes avoided mine, as I felt his body stiffen when I tried to touch him. I wanted to throw myself into the overflowing river for my idiocy, I wanted to yell at myself for the thousandth time in my life to keep my stupid mouth shut, but I probably wouldn't have listened anyway.

I sneaked up to his room while he was downstairs watching TV, and stole some Internet time. The fact he didn't come looking for me spoke volumes. Well. I'd accused him of murder, and then as good as admitted it myself. What did I expect, a forgiving peck on the cheek? More than likely he couldn't bear to touch me. He could touch a fat cleric's rotting corpse, I thought, anger burning my throat and eyes. But he couldn't touch me.

I could barely see the desktop's blurred screen, I had to keep blinking hard to make it out at all, but I managed to locate the search engine and type in 'amnesia'. But so many sites were blocked, especially the medical ones, it was impossible to know which were any good, and the connection kept being interrupted. They might not be able to control the Internet but they were having a pretty good stab at it.

Memory loss, retrograde amnesia, transient global amnesia. I never knew it was so complicated. I never knew there were so many kinds. How long did it last? The answer was different everywhere I looked. Could it come back in patches? On and off? Riddle me this.

I'd hit my head on the tarmac, I'd fractured my skull. Could I still be having blackouts? I'd made myself forget what happened in the vestry when I was eleven. Could I be good at that now? Four years' practice. Could I be getting better at suppressing my memories, like I was getting better at lying? Was it a learned skill? Could I make myself forget something else?

Could I kill somebody and forget I'd done it?

Nobody would tell me, so I just sat and stared at the screen and cried for a while, then logged off. I didn't dare go down to Ming. I didn't want to feel that coldness coming off him like I was opening a freezer door. I didn't want to endure Keyser Soze's smug leer as he curled possessively on Ming's lap, Ming's fingers rubbing his skull between his ears, when it was my scalp that needed stroking.

The worst part was, I could sense my own desperation, so I'm sure Ming could too. I was practically throwing myself at him, and I knew I was doing it, but I couldn't stop myself. That night we lay in his bed, because we didn't want to admit to ourselves that anything was wrong, but we quickly found that even in a single bed two people could lie all night without touching each other.

If we'd slept simultaneously we might have rolled together without meaning to, our bodies pulled together like magnets, and that might have been enough to crack the sheet ice between us and make us like each other again. But at no point were we both deeply asleep. When we were exhausted enough we dozed in turn, one at a time like sentries, but all we were guarding against was each other. I just wanted to melt into him again, so he'd make me feel better like he always had, but all of a sudden we were chemically incompatible. We woke to a surly, monosyllabic morning.

Mum picked a good time to show up, then.

She must have sensed the atmosphere in the house as soon as Ming opened the door to her, because she glanced first at him and then at me, hanging back in the dimness of the hallway, and said, 'Are you okay, Cassie?'

I nodded, then realising she couldn't see me well I said, 'Yes. Hi, Mum.'

Mum turned to Ming, her brow furrowing. 'Can I have a word with your mother?'

Ming managed not to shoot me a glance. 'She's out,' he said smoothly. 'They both are.'

Mum watched his eyes.

'They'll be back in a couple of hours if you want to wait.' He shrugged.

I was chilled by his nerve, but Mum smiled more naturally and shook her head. 'No, Menzies, it's okay. I want to talk to Cass and I think we need to go for a walk.'

I bit a thumbnail, ripping it carefully off with my teeth. 'How's Abby?'

'I don't know.' The smile grew brighter, less natural. 'Dad's seeing her, Cass. She's okay just now, so far as I know.'

I swallowed hard. 'Are they treating her all right?'

'Yes. Yes, Cassie, they are. She hasn't been charged with anything yet.'

'Oh,' I said. 'Hasn't she?'

The edge in my tone must have cut through to Mum.

Twisting her hands together, she bent the fingers so far backwards I reached for them, terrified they'd break. When she saw my movement she took a breath and looked up, and I snatched my own hands back.

'Cassie.' She sucked her lower lip. 'Your Dad.'

'What about him?'

'Do you remember, Cass, when you woke up one morning with a spider on your face? A big one.' She made a wry face, trying to make a joke of it though the memory still made my spine tingle. Anyway, didn't she know my sense of humour was on extended leave? 'I think you were seven or eight,' she said. 'You just woke up and found it there, remember?'

Oh, like I'd forget.

'You were demented. I would be too!' she added hurriedly. 'Your Dad had to chase it round the room till he killed it. He didn't really like killing them, but he knew you'd never sleep again if he didn't get it.'

Yeah. I gave her a reluctant smile.

'And your Dad hugged you and said he'd never let another monster near you. He'd never let a monster touch you again. Do you remember that?'

'Yes,' I said, looking at the wall.

'Well.' Mum hesitated. 'It's just that he was wrong. He couldn't keep the monster away and he couldn't even chase it down afterwards.'

Ming just stood there, but he didn't seem embarrassed at all. He listened and said nothing.

'And I know that's not your fault, it's his and mine. But please, Cass, just think, promise me once every day you'll think how your father feels about that.'

Bad Faith

I turned my head and stared at the door, wishing I could barge it down and run away.

Mum put her knuckles to her eyes. 'I'm ready to tell you why Abby's in jail. But only if you're ready to hear it.'

I looked at Ming, and he looked at me, and then at Mum. And Mum just looked at me.

'I'll be in my room,' said Ming.

17: Holy Joe

'They knew who Holy Joe was. They knew all along.'

The coffee in Mum's cardboard cup was stone cold because all she'd done was turn it in her fingers, her shoulders hunched over as if she was trying to protect it from the dripping tree above our bench. The rain had eased but it hadn't stopped, and water trickled and rolled from her wet hair to her jaw before running down her neck, bypassing her upturned collar. She must be getting soaked. The massive sycamore wasn't much shelter. I suppose I was getting soaked too.

'He could have been stopped, Cass, because somebody knew him. How else could they have known that body they found was Holy Joe's? It had been there so long, so long. Someone must have identified him. From clothes, maybe, or a piece of jewellery. Or they had his dental records. So you see, someone knew him. We were right about that. Terribly right. So we did the right thing, you see, Cass? We did the right thing all along.'

'Mum,' I said. 'What did you do?'

We sat at opposite ends of the bench, tetchy gulls screaming above our heads, and watched litter bob in a scummy rim round the park boating lake, pockmarked with rain. I tried to take another mouthful of coffee but got only the last oily dregs. Mum's lashes were dewed with rainwater, and she rubbed them with a fist to clear them.

'Oh, Cassandra, I'm sorry I was useless after Abby was

arrested. I don't know why I froze up and couldn't tell you everything. I've had enough time to think about it.'

'Well,' I said, though I tried to restrain myself. 'You're used to not telling me stuff.'

'I know. I'm sorry I've been no use to you for the last four years. We're too used to secrets in our family, too used to secrets and death and saying nothing.'

She was babbling, prevaricating, and she knew it.

'You know about Holy Joe but you don't remember him, you don't remember the fear. It was like a virus. Nobody really thought it would be them next – nobody ever does – but nobody felt safe. It wasn't as if we thought they'd find him and stop him. There were people, *church* people, who said they understood him, that his heart was in the right place. The right place! Cass, can you imagine? Oh, he was trying to save those women's souls. He was trying to push back the permissive society; well, wasn't the One Church trying to do the same? Sure, he was disturbed, he was going about things the wrong way, but *his aims were holy*. He was devout. He *meant well*. Those girls were asking for it. Oh, Cassie.' There were real tears in Mum's eyes now, but she didn't rub them away. 'They weren't asking for it any more than you were.'

A cold-eyed gull skidded onto the water and folded its wings, bright snowy white against the greenish murk. Out of nowhere, I wanted to cry for those murdered girls. I wondered how they'd felt, I wondered if they'd managed to blank it out, any of it, or if they knew everything about their own deaths. Ferociously I chewed the edge of my coffee cup.

'We were looking the wrong way, so we were. We worried and fretted and looked over our shoulders for Holy Joe, while Ma Baxter got into politics. Ma Baxter wasn't a bogeyman.'

'She makes people feel safe,' I said with sudden clarity.

'That's true.' Mum stirred her coffee with a fingertip. 'People scare their children with bug-eyed monsters, not Ma Baxter and militias. People like a bit of repression, you know.'

'So long as they're not getting it themselves,' I put in bitterly, thinking of Ming.

'Yes. Do you blame them? Ma Baxter feeds people's fears, Cass, and then she feeds off them. She terrifies you with the monster under the bed, then she offers to kill it for you. The Church let her use them but they knew what they were doing, and they used her too. Politics and extreme religion: what a cocktail! We all got drunk on it and we've still got the hangover.'

'That's one of Dad's lines.'

Mum laughed shakily. 'Yes.'

'Abby says it can't last forever. The One Church.'

'Maybe not. Maybe it'll collapse under the weight of its own conflicts, but my, it'll get ugly in the meantime. They'll do their damnedest to wipe out secularism and atheism before it does the same to them. Your father thinks the Church needs to split to stop it becoming a monster. Wilf thinks that'll kill it. Who's to know who's right?' Mum poured her cold coffee into the wet grass, then looked longingly towards the coffee kiosk.

'Don't even think about it, Mum,' I said. 'You didn't drink the last one.'

'Ah, I know. I'm putting it off, getting away from Holy

Joe. Maybe I'm scared of him even now. I see him in my dreams, Cass, I see him before I fall asleep. Didn't we all?'

Oh, bad dreams, guilty dreams. I knew about those.

'But you did see him, Mum?'

'Yes, Cassie. I saw him. For real.' Mum heaved a sigh. 'Like I said, nobody thinks it'll happen to them, but everybody's afraid it'll happen to someone they know. I was afraid for Abby, her and her boyfriends and her hairdos and her dancing and her makeup. My mother used to try and scare her with tales of Holy Joe, what he'd do when he found her kissing a boy.'

'And wasn't she scared?' I shivered.

'Abby? You're joking. She didn't exactly laugh in your grandmother's face, God knows she'd never dare do that, but she sniggered and giggled in our bedroom in the dark. I used to lie there frozen to the mattress, terrified Bunty would think we were both laughing behind her back. I don't know who scared me more: Holy Joe, or Bunty.'

'Bunty.' I made a wry face.

'Ah, well. You weren't there, you didn't feel the fear. Mind you, nor did Abby, the silly cow.' Tipping her head back, Mum closed her eyes and let water drip onto her skin from the sagging foliage. 'She went too far one night, our Abby. Probably in a lot of senses, because she was out much too late, and Bunty stayed up to wait for her. Oh, I shivered in our bedroom, wondering what Bunty would do when Abby showed up. Abby was a trial to her, she kept saying, a trial. The Cross the Lord had sent her. And see, I was more nervous than ever for Abby, because that night we were the only people left in the whole building, in the whole *square*. We were last to leave before the renovations and there'd be no neighbours to intervene on Abby's behalf. Lord knows everybody interfered in everyone else's business all the time, but not that night. Everyone else was gone.' She put the palms of her hands over her eyes. 'You never really knew those tenements, Cass, but you've seen them. Can you picture Bunty's?'

'Four flights up,' I said. 'That tiny square of yard with a drying green at the back. Buildings all round. And Dad took me up the close once. It was narrow and the stairs were bare stone. No carpet but it had those gorgeous green tiles halfway up the walls.'

'That's right.' Mum dropped her hands to smile at me. 'Four flights up, and it must have been a health and safety risk because Bunty had her sash windows up and down so often, they could open themselves. If she wasn't flinging the window up to shout some gossip to a neighbour, she was eavesdropping on somebody else's, or yelling at rowdy kids with a football. God, we didn't need mobile phones in those days, Cass. We just opened a window.'

I grinned.

'Ah, but we loved it. It was the size of a cupboard, so it was, but I miss that flat. And Bunty had the window open that night, that's how she heard the noise. So would half the neighbourhood, if they'd been there. It was still the old government back then, and they were getting desperate, spending a fortune for our votes. What they could afford, anyway. So they were moving everyone out while they revamped the flats. Our upstairs neighbours moved out the day before, the next door lot were long gone, and we were due to move out a few days later. Holy Joe must have thought the place was empty. Must have, or he'd never have brought the girl there. He couldn't have known Bunty was listening for her trollop of a daughter, all the lights out, waiting to thrash her. He'd have approved of that! Almost funny, isn't it?'

'Almost,' I said.

She nodded. 'Bunty had ears like a bat, so she'd hardly miss a clatter and a muffled cry in the close, where it opened onto the back yard. And I wasn't asleep, I crept through and watched her bend down and glare out the window but she never opened it further to lean out. It squeaked, though it was opened a million times a day, and she didn't want them to know she was coming for them like the Avenging Angel of the Lord. She thought it was Abby, you see.'

'But it wasn't.'

'No, but Abby did her hair the same way as that wretched girl, and the light was poor down there. Now, Bunty could move like a very well-built cat when she wanted to. She wedged the door of the flat open, because it banged if you left it, and she tiptoed down the stairs. Stone stairs that didn't creak, wouldn't betray a mother stalking her errant daughter with a rolling pin.'

'Rolling pin,' I echoed.

'Honestly, Cass. Like something out of the *Beano*. I was right behind her and I wanted to laugh and I wanted to shout and warn Abby, but I didn't dare, and just as well. Bunty crept up on what she thought was Abby, and I think she really would have given her a hiding.'

'What happened? When she saw it wasn't Abby?'

'Oh, Bunty had her wits about her, thank God. She was

no fool. My mother knew the difference between sex and strangulation, even in a bad light.' Mum bit her lip, as if she'd got carried away and said too much. I wanted to snap at her, *I'm fifteen, Mother. What do you think I don't know?* But I didn't want to open that can of worms.

'My mother beat Holy Joe to death with a rolling pin, Cass.'

I was neither as shocked nor as horrified as I ought to be. Somehow it seemed perfectly reasonable behaviour. It's in the genes.

A gull screeched, squabbling over a sodden crust, and Mum shook herself back to the moment. 'First one blow, that got him turning with shock in his eyes. Pale, brilliant eyes, Cass; I hope you never see anything like them.' She drew in a breath with the memory. 'And then another blow, and another, because his shock had turned into rage and she was frightened. And then she hit him again, and I suppose it was just harder and harder to stop.' She was staring at nothing, as if she was back there and watching it all over again. 'She'd gone too far, and besides, she'd seen what he was doing. Bunty had a sense of justice, Cass, and a temper. Oh Lord, she had a temper.

'Abby walked into the close as we were standing over him, and Gabriel was with her 'cause she'd met him on the way. Your father walked her home because he was that besotted with me, he wanted to impress my sister. Bless him.'

I chucked my cardboard cup into the lake. Being a litter-bug didn't seem so bad. The rain pattered on it, spun and turned it. It drifted, grew waterlogged and sank.

'Lucky for Abby Bunty had spent all her temper on Holy

Joe, and anyway we had other things to think about. The girl was sobbing like a banshee but Bunty just told her to shut up, and let me tell you, when Bunty told you to shut up you did, and no questions asked.'

'I know. I remember.' I wished I had my cup back to chew on. 'Didn't you tell anyone?'

Mum looked askance at me. 'What? We knew the rumour, that Holy Joe had friends in dangerous places. We were half-crazy with fear. We weren't going to hand over our mother to explain herself to the police. And if it had been the militias? To them he was Robin Hood, Cass, he was a hero. They'd have shot us in the back of the neck and put us in an unmarked grave. Do you think I'm exaggerating?'

I picked at my fingernails, not wanting to answer. The truth was, I didn't want to understand. I didn't want to think my mother had done the right thing, the only thing. But that was just my mood, and it would pass. I knew she had. They all had.

'There was a poky wee flat next door to us, the landowner had crammed it in, in Victorian times. Well, the council had decided to knock it through, split the space between the other two flats on that floor. So they were bricking up its old chimney and putting in modern radiators and a new electric stove. They'd just about finished closing off the chimney so we got Holy Joe into a big old suitcase, and we wrapped it up in lots of black plastic bags and taped it up, and stuck him in the chimney space. Gabriel spent all night bricking him in. He did a good job, that's for sure, because there was never a smell, or never a noticeable one, and if we imagined an odour we'd just open the window.' Lamely she said: 'We were always opening the window...'

'Mum,' I said, rubbing my temples. 'Mum, wasn't there blood?'

'Oh, yes, blood and brains. Quite a lot. But next morning Bunty was out there before six, scrubbing the step and the tiles. We were moving out, but she always did that, and if anyone saw her they'd have thought it was perfectly normal. We were house-proud in those days.'

'House-proud,' I echoed. I had a terrible urge to laugh. 'What was Dad thinking?'

'Your father...

Look, Holy Joe was a serial killer. He was a brute, Cass, an animal. Worse than an animal. Those girls he murdered, who did they ever hurt?' She glared at me, daring me to argue. I wasn't there, after all. I never felt the fear.

'Of course your father had doubts! But Bunty swore him to silence, told him she'd hunt him down and rolling-pin him to death like Holy Joe if he ever breathed a word – and by the way he could forget about marrying me if he did. But Bunty liked things done right, and she asked Gabriel to read the last rites over the bricked-up chimney. So he did.'

I could picture that. Holy Joe wouldn't have troubled Dad's conscience; he'd have kept his mind on the girls. He'd be perfectly happy with what he'd done, and perfectly happy with reading the rites. Religion. It's a get-out clause. Maybe sometimes there's a good reason for that.

'The girl, she was Abby's best friend's...'

'Boyfriend's sister? Coincidence, love. Irrelevant. We never knew that till later. Poor child: she was so grateful for not being dead she'd have agreed to anything. We cleaned her up and gave her tea and cheap whisky to settle her nerves, and she swore never to say a word about it. She wore a scarf to hide the bruises and she kept her mouth shut. Do you think she wanted the militias on her heels, any more than we did?'

'But people knew,' I protested. 'I used to tell the story at school. He walked her home and he disappeared when he saw other people and...'

'Uh-huh. People saw her and Holy Joe together, of course they did. Well, they thought he looked awful like Holy Joe's description. But she'd survived, and by the time the story got around to the police, and inevitably to the militias, the bruises had faded. When folk asked, she said the man had walked her home, right enough. But he'd drifted away.' Mum turned into a fluttery mimic, high-pitched and panicky. *'That nice man was Holy Joe, but? Really do you think so? Holy God, I'll be down on my knees to thank the good Lord for my deliverance.* How could anyone say it was otherwise?'

I stared at the greasy surface of the boating lake, pitted and dappled with rain. It was heavier again, worsening, bouncing off the water and the tarmac path, and the patter of it on the sycamore leaves had turned to a drumming. Mum's hair and clothes were drenched. So were mine, I realised with shock.

'The last known sighting of Holy Joe,' I said.

'Yes. Till they knocked down the tenement last week and found him.'

18: The Return of Todd

When I pushed open the bedroom door Ming was lying on his bed staring at the ceiling, hands clasped on his chest like a dead mediaeval knight, except his eyes were open and his feet were bare and instead of a hound lying at them, there was a fat complacent cat.

He didn't even bother to look at me. Righteous fury constricted my throat again.

'I'll come back later,' I said coldly. 'Unless you don't want me to.'

'Cass!'

I turned back. There was alarm in the way he'd said my name, but now his eyes were closed, as if he'd given himself away a little.

'What?' I said.

'Come here,' he mumbled.

'Say again? I didn't *catch that*.'

'Come here,' he moaned again, '*please*.'

That's better, I wanted to say, but I couldn't quite get it out. Conflicting impulses were battling it out in my brain and my heart, because I was still furious with him.

Ming had opened his eyes and rolled his head round, and if there's a girl on earth who could have resisted the spaniel look he gave me, I'd like to know how. Of course, most of the girls on earth weren't fanatically in love with him against their better judgment.

'I'm sorry,' he said.

'Okay, then.' I flopped onto the bed beside him.

He rolled over and put his arms round me. 'I'm sorry,' he whispered. 'I wanted to be angry with you because life would be easier. I wanted to be angry so I could be on my own again and curl up and be miserable and not be responsible for you. All right? So I made myself angry. You didn't do anything wrong. I said I'd have liked to do it, didn't I? I'd have liked to kill him, and I know fine you didn't. So that's that.'

'How do you know I didn't kill him?' I said. 'I don't.'

'Yeah, you do. You know you didn't do that. You couldn't kill a spider, Cass.'

We just looked at each other, then spluttered with nervous laughter.

'Okay, bad example. Spiders and rabbits, that's all. You couldn't kill a person, Cass, not even in your sleep.'

If Ming thought that was true, it was all that mattered. Right or wrong, his was the only opinion I cared for right now. I didn't even care for mine. Actually I was afraid of my own opinion.

'Do you still want to be on your own? Do you still want me to go away?' I was afraid of Ming's answer.

'No,' he said, blinking at me, 'cause I thought you were going to, there, for a minute. And I really, really changed my mind. Okay?'

I smiled. 'Okay.'

'What about your aunt? What's the Holy Joe thing?'

'Um.' I stroked the side of his face with my forefinger. 'Okay. Well, my grandmother murdered the old psycho because he was strangling some girl in her close. So Abby and Mum and Dad hid the body. Stuffed him in a hole

and bricked him up. Now they've knocked down the tenements and the demolition workers have found him.' I gave
Ming a bright Tanya-Moonfleet smile. 'Holy Joe, that is.'

Ming looked at me for absolutely ages. He took a breath
occasionally, or opened his mouth like he was going to
start asking questions, but obviously the questions were
inadequate, because each time he shut his mouth again
and frowned.

'Um,' he said at last. 'Fine.'

'Aunt Abby insisted on taking the whole blame, apparently. She's told the police Mum was asleep in bed that
night and Dad was nowhere near the place. She told them
the truth about Bunty killing him and why she did it. And
how she helped hide the body.' I nestled my head into the
pillow, still following the contours of Ming's face with my
finger. 'When the redevelopment started, they all realised
the body was bound to turn up. That's why they've been
so antsy about it. Abby said to Dad that Bunty's dead and
gone, and she doesn't have kids herself, so why shouldn't
she take the blame? They argued with her till they were
blue and pink in the face but she wouldn't take no for an
answer.'

Ming put his hand over mine against his face, and curled
his fingers round it. 'What's going to happen to her?'

'I don't know. Ma Baxter's not going to make a big political issue out of him, she's not stupid. The militias loved
him, but he was a serial killer! Who's going to want justice
for him? He's already got it!'

'Ah,' intoned Ming, 'but he was very much the People's
Psychopath.'

I giggled, not quite deciphering the look in his eyes.

'Community service for Abby, Dad reckons, and a criminal record, but no jail. Be ironic if she's put to work down the Laundries.'

Ming sighed, took my ear lightly between thumb and forefinger and wriggled close for a kiss. 'You'll be joining her there if anybody catches you doing this.'

'What?'

'This.'

'Oh.' I curled my body happily against his. 'This!'

• • •

'I'll get some toast,' mumbled Ming.

I wasn't arguing. While he pulled on his jeans I snuggled under the duvet, liking the way his jeans sat on his hips, and the vertebrae in the small of his back, and his shoulder blades, and the long muscles down either side of his spine. I liked most things about him. No, everything.

When he was gone, I reached for the remote with the tips of my fingers. I made a game of it, letting as little of myself as possible touch the cool air. I was enjoying the enfolding warmth of the duvet and the contrast of it with the batter of rain against the window. Actually I shouldn't need the remote at all; in the tiny bedroom the antiquated little television was jammed up close by the bed, and if I weren't so lazy and cosy I'd just reach right out and press a button.

I snatched the remote into my cocoon, ducked my head under the duvet, then opened a tiny tunnel onto the world to click on the TV. I was hoping for *Angels and Martyrs* but it was the news again. Must be an extended edition. I was about to click it off again when Ma Baxter appeared at her podium. She managed to make her black designer dress look like something anybody's grandma might wear. But only in deepest mourning.

Her eyes, dark raisins in her pudding-face, were hard and determined, and her fingers gripped the podium as if she was only just managing to contain her righteous wrath.

'Our worst fears are confirmed,' she said. There was a well-judged break in her voice, just the right degree of grief to show she was bravely overcoming her devastation. 'But he has come back to us after all this time, even in death, to help us track down his killers. We owe him that.' Swallowing, she closed her eyes. '*I owe him that.*'

I shoved off the duvet and knelt up in bed. I couldn't be that wrong, could I? She couldn't use Holy Joe for a sympathy magnet, she *couldn't.*

'All our hopes and prayers have come to nothing. Now all we can do is pray for his soul, safe in the care of God.' Raisin-eyes glittered in the pop of flashbulbs. 'And find the monsters responsible for this appalling crime.'

A sound at the bedroom door made my head jerk round. Ming was standing there, pale and drawn as death, a tray in his hands with two mugs on it and a toast rack. I don't know why I was crying but I was. Even through my tears I could see the toast rack was empty, he'd forgotten the toast. Behind the sound of the vengeful screaming mob on television, I could hear the burble of the kitchen radio from the room below.

Ming's hands shook, and coffee was slopping onto the tray, but his voice was perfectly level and calm.

'He's washed downstream. Todd's been found.'

And then the phone rang.

19: Weather Change

The rain had stopped. Finally. That was sod's law, I thought bitterly. Wasn't life full of these little ironies?

Mum and I stood under the dripping rowan above the river valley. Above us the clouds were ripping and fraying like an old shroud, letting patches of watery sunlight spill through. Where the weak rays lit the trees in the gorge, they glowed with fresh summery green. The whole world was brightening and clearing, the sky lifting away from the earth. Atmospherically speaking, it was all very inappropriate.

Only the river was as it should be, churning and raging, still well beyond its banks. Some smaller trees had been dislodged, smashed top-first into the brown torrent.

Somebody had to say something. I guess it had to be me. 'Dad's lost his faith, hasn't he?'

'Yes,' said Mum. 'Don't ever repeat that, will you? Especially not now.'

I licked my lips. Poor Dad. 'Does anyone else know?'

'Only Wilf. Apostasy is a serious matter, Cass.' She sighed. 'Maybe it's like Griff said. Maybe all he's lost is his religion.'

'That's semantics, isn't it?' What a cynic I was turning into. 'It doesn't matter what you call it. That's just a game.' *QUIT GAME?*

Mum dealt with that in the traditional family way: she changed the subject.

'Ming's parents aren't home, are they?' she said. 'They're in jail. Long term.'

RESUME.

I didn't say anything. I didn't need to. I was still worried about leaving Ming in the house with Dad, who beat people to death with rocks when they touched his daughter.

'You lied to me, Cass.'

'Yes,' I said.

I didn't say another word. I didn't have to. I think she took my point.

Mum sighed again, but she didn't sound angry, just tired. 'You'll have to come home, Cass. Please.' Taking a breath, she added, 'Ming must come too. He can't stay there on his own.'

'He does it all the time.' I shrugged.

'It's different now. It's not safe. Have you watched the news? They're whipping up the mobs. An Assembly member was beaten up in the street for suggesting Todd's death might have been an accident. He said there was no proof of foul play, that Todd might have slipped and fallen in by himself. That won't do, of course. They want someone to pay.'

I started to shiver, and couldn't stop. Wrapping my arms around my body, I hugged it tightly. My mother was silent for a very long time.

'Cass,' she said at last, my name croaky as if it had fallen out of use and she couldn't remember how to use it. 'Cass, if I ever have to go away…'

'Don't you dare!' Suddenly I was screaming at her, I couldn't help myself. 'Don't say that! That's what Abby said! Why would you have to go away? If you've got some other secret just tell me! I can't stand another surprise, okay? You tell me!'

She looked so shocked you'd think it was odd that I'd want to be kept informed. I almost hated her for a second.

'You think I like not knowing things?' I yelled. 'Sometimes I feel like I don't know anything! I don't even know any more what I've done! I can't remember!'

'But you...'

'Mum, there's a whole month or more still gone. I don't remember my eleventh birthday.' I swallowed tears. 'There's voices in my head, how's that ever good? Maybe they told me to do stuff. Maybe I still have blackouts. How would I know?' My voice rose in pitch, uncontrollable. 'I'm always down in the ghost wood! How do I know I didn't kill Todd? *Me!*'

Mum stared at me, terrified. She said, 'How do you know he died in that wood?'

'Because I... because I...' I didn't know how to tell her, I just didn't. And suddenly that wasn't what was worrying me. My throat tightened.

'Mum. Mum. How do *you?*'

To give her credit, she didn't look away. She smiled a meaningless motherly smile that was meant to reassure me, and then she said, 'The same way I know you didn't kill Todd.'

I wanted her to stop talking now. But I couldn't speak to shut her up.

'I know you didn't, Cass. I know that because I killed him myself.'

• • •

'I saw him walking on the road, right past our house. I thought it was such unbelievable, God-given luck, seeing him go up that way alone, and I had the most desperate need to follow him. To talk to him. That's all, Cass, I swear it, I didn't go meaning to harm him. I wanted to hear him say sorry for what he'd done to you, to all of us, but of all the stupid mundane things, I couldn't find my boots. In the end I grabbed your Dad's, but they're too big and I had to rummage around for thick socks. By the time I ran after Todd, he'd gone quite a way. He's a fast walker. I didn't catch him up till he was at that disused track, the one that goes into your ghost wood.'

'Oh,' I said. Picking up a twig, I began to shred the bark from it. We sat together on Mum's waterproof jacket, watching the roaring river and not seeing it. Mum had her arms wrapped round her knees, leaning slightly forward, so there wasn't actually any physical contact between us, but I felt closer to my mother than I had in years.

She sighed, blinking. 'It all started spilling out of me straight away, but you could see Todd was panicking. He kept glancing around, like he was afraid someone might hear what I was saying. It's a quiet road, but cars do go past. One did go by, as we were standing there, but who-ever it was hasn't ever come forward. Anyway, after that Todd really got antsy. He said, look, come off the road. So we did. We walked down the ghost wood track, and once we were out of sight of the road we just kept going, because I couldn't stop talking. I talked and talked. I think I was crying. And I thought he was listening, I really did. I truly thought I was getting through to him, Cass. I thought even now I could forgive him, if he'd only say sorry.'

'It wasn't up to you to forgive him,' I said. The words were out before I could think.

She didn't quite meet my eyes. 'I know that. I know it now, and I'm sorry. But I thought whatever else he was, Todd was a man of God. He must have a conscience, he must be afraid of his own judgement day. That's what kept me going.' Mum laughed without a trace of humour. 'Being that scared would be a punishment in itself.'

Passing the buck to God, I thought, but I didn't blame her. If you couldn't do that, maybe the world would drive you mad.

'He hadn't a shred of remorse,' she said bleakly. 'Your father told me that. But when I realised it was true? I thought all the air had been knocked out of my lungs. Todd didn't think he'd ever be punished, not even in the next life. He told me to give it up, because who'd believe your father now? Not only was it too late to throw accusations, things had changed. Who'd believe your father about *anything?*'

I waited in silence, knowing there was worse to come.

'He knew, you see. Todd knew Gabriel had lost his faith. He said if I knew what was good for me and my family, I'd go home and forget all this.' Mum frowned, shaking her head as if she still didn't believe her ears. 'He actually told me to *forget it.*'

I leaned my head against her shoulder. 'Maybe you should. You did your best.'

Mum gave a cynical chuckle. 'The smirk on Todd's fat face! He reminded me it wasn't just Gabriel's job that was at stake. Did I know the criminal penalty for apostasy? Did I know the ecclesiastical one? Well, of course I did. It was one more hold he'd have over Gabriel, one more stick to beat him with, but I still didn't understand it, I didn't understand how a Bishop could tolerate an apostate in his diocese. See what I'm getting at, Cass? I was shocked Todd knew, but I was even more shocked that he'd done nothing about it. I asked how he knew about Gabriel's apostasy and he said *Don't you think I know what a man looks like who's lost his faith?* And he laughed and said, *I see one every morning in my bathroom mirror.*'

'Oh, my God,' I breathed.

'He'd never admit it, of course. Lose his position, his power, his celebrity? Lose that army of youths who worship him? Never. In a way he was as trapped as your father.

'I told him I was sorry. I know how tortured your father is by his loss of faith, and I thought it was like that for Todd, too. He just looked at me with those cold eyes and smiled, and I realised he didn't give a damn. Not a damn. He had Gabriel at his mercy, he could ruin him at any moment by exposing him, but the fact he was an apostate himself meant nothing to him. It was only politics. He could fake it. And we couldn't threaten him with exposure in return, because nobody would ever believe me or your father. Not in a thousand years.'

What must it have been like? I knew how it felt, that rage that fills you up, like trying to pour too much water into a glass. You just can't do it. You can't stop it spilling. Poor Mum.

I pressed closer, till she leaned back and put an arm round me. 'How did you...'

'He turned his back on me, Cass. He told me to forget it, and he turned his back on me. That's what I couldn't bear. It was so… contemptuous.' She stared down into the gorge.

I swallowed. 'Spur of the moment thing, then?'

'He'd moved down the slope, trying to get away from me. I'd followed. We were at the bottom of the slope and I was a little above him. And he *dismissed* me, like all he cared about was watching the river. He practically… he practically…'

Asked for it. I stared at her. Shamefaced, she averted her eyes, and didn't say it.

'There were stones at my feet, big river stones, as if someone had put them there just for me. My head was spinning with hate. I didn't think, couldn't think, I could barely see for hatred. I picked one up and slammed it into the side of his head. He went down like a… down like a…'

'Stone,' I said. That part must have been easy, impulsive. I tried to picture the next bit, the bit where she slammed the stone down again and again, but my mind wouldn't let me.

'Oh, Cass.' Mum looked dreamily into the middle distance. 'I'd already been involved in violent death, hadn't I? I didn't wield that rolling pin, but I covered for my mother, Abby and I both did. I manhandled a broken corpse into a suitcase and stuffed it in a hole in the wall. It hardens you, Cass, over time. It just does, when there's no way to confess, no way to get the poison out of your soul. If Todd had known that, he might not have made such a terrible misjudgement, but he didn't know. A terrible mistake. His last mistake.'

I sat there letting chills run up and down my spine, but Mum was calm.

'I didn't panic straight away. I didn't feel anything as I walked away, but when I came back to the track it dawned on me what I'd done, and I ran. I crossed the road and went up to the steading and went home that way. No-one saw me. Except your Dad. I thought he was at his meeting but he'd been walking up on the hill and he saw me cross the road. He can always read my mind. He nagged me for days, till I told him everything, and then he was as scared for me as I was for him. He went to the wood, but by that time the body was gone.'

I thought I'd better keep my mouth shut at this point.

'Todd must have drowned when the water rose.' She shrugged. 'Got washed away. Maybe he got stuck underwater for a while, but I knew he'd come back, I've been waiting, and they're bound to trace it to me. Your Dad wants to take responsibility. He says he's a One Church cleric and they'll let him off lightly, but I know that isn't true. It'd be worse for him. *Much* worse. I won't let him take the blame, so I wanted to warn you. And explain, so you don't think too badly of me. Because if I'm arrested, I may not get another chance to talk to you.'

All I could do was stare at her. She felt empty under my touch, as if I could nudge her and she'd simply blow away into the gorge like tumbleweed. My own head was so full it ached, and I shook it and shook it till I'd shaken it to the top, that thing she'd said that was all wrong.

'Mum,' I said. 'He didn't drown, Mum. How can you think that?'

'Oh, Cassie, he was alive when I left him. I could have

gone for help and I should have.' She put her head in her hands. 'I could have pulled him away from the water. But I didn't. I let him die.'

I started to laugh then, I couldn't help it, and Mum stared at me as if I'd gone mad. She looked hurt, and bewildered, and so frightened for me that I started to feel bad. So though I wanted to go on laughing, I made myself stop, and we sat there in electric silence.

'Cass,' she said in a trembling voice, 'you haven't told me.'

'What?' I said.

'You haven't told me how you knew. How you knew he was in the wood.'

'Same way I know he didn't drown, Mum. You didn't kill him.' I gave her a happy inappropriate grin. 'Somebody got there after you. He'd a hole in his skull the size of a fist.'

20: Don't Look Back

'Jeez, I bet that took some explaining,' said Ming. 'How you knew that.'

'Not half.' I grinned at him.

We were both a bit out of breath, having run and dodged, giggling, halfway from my home. Griff was still stalking us. Hard habit to break, I guess.

'Think we shook him off?' Slipping his hand into mine as we walked on, Ming glanced back.

'I think so. Poor Griff. We could just have waited for him. Now we know he isn't going to kill you.'

'Yeah, I know.' His fingers tightened on mine. 'But I want you to myself for a bit. It's not like we'll get left on our own once I'm staying at your house.'

I laughed. 'Not ever again. Mum's just mad as hell. She doesn't want to fall out with me, but she won't take her eyes off us.'

'I'll have to suck up to her like mad. Do the dishes every night. How much slave labour will make up for your chastity?'

That made me laugh again, but I was still glad to be going home. It would feel safer and far more normal than Ming's. I had only my backpack to pick up, and Ming didn't want to take much: a few changes of clothes and his toothbrush, and Keyser Soze of course. God knew what we were going to do with him. I had a notion involving a syringe and some merciful barbiturates, but I supposed we'd have to give the brute house room for a while.

We could have asked Dad to drive us to Ming's place (no, he hadn't battered Ming to death; indeed Ming said he was pretty civilised, given the circumstances) but we needed the air. Somehow, after the saturated days that had gone before, the air was breathable again, and we wanted to breathe it, make our heads float with it. The absence of lashing endless rain made you grin whether you felt like it or not.

Besides, I still felt absurdly happy at clearing my mother of any wrongdoing except for hitting Todd on the head with a stone and knocking him out. And let's face it: who wouldn't?

The only trouble was, it meant I wasn't off the hook myself. Nor, strictly speaking, was Dad. But somehow I felt lighter of heart than I had for weeks. I was losing my cosy existence with Ming, but I was losing my guilty conscience about it, too (oh, that upbringing of mine). And he was coming home to stay with us for a while. That was even better.

Even Griff's presence wouldn't be too oppressive, since these days he seemed to want to live and let live. He still kept an eye on us, but a protective one. And we were still good at giving him the slip. Like now.

'I heard from my cousin,' said Ming.

'That means you're really going,' I said. I kept my voice as level as I could. No point making a fuss; this might be Ming's idea but it wasn't his fault. One of these days he'd be back. Why make it harder for him in the meantime?

'Uh-huh. If I can get across the border and call him, he'll pick me up and give me a place to live. Try and find me a job. Handle my asylum application. He says they might not even intern me, if I stay at his place and report every day. It won't be so bad, Cass. Better than here.'

I chewed my cheek. 'Will you get over the border okay?'

'Yeah. The government can't focus on the border while there's so much else happening. Did you hear? They're trying to root out the secularist bases on the islands again, and there's uproar in the Assembly. Two members have been arrested.'

'Yeah, I know.' I still couldn't get too excited about politics.

'So I'll go south and I'll slip across the border at night. There's wild places. People who help. I'll miss you, Cass. Wait for me?'

He slipped it in quite casually, and he didn't even sound too optimistic about my answer.

'Course I will,' I told him, a little crossly because there was no need for him to ask, and it kept me from crying.

So he squeezed my hand, and that was that. It was a contract.

We walked in contented silence, a whole street. The nicest walk of my life, and one I'll remember on my deathbed. Ming's lips were moving slightly, and I knew he was just singing to himself in absolute silence. He used to do that when he was much younger and I used to amuse myself trying to guess the song. I was almost never right.

I was still watching him, sidelong, as we turned the corner. That's why I saw his mouth form an obscenity, and I heard it clearly when he said it again out loud. He was staring ahead. I didn't want to, I knew that from the look in his eyes, but I followed his gaze anyway.

There were people milling about, bodies hunched, a madness in the air. Others were hurrying past, panic in every taut angle of their bodies, pretending not to see. A single cop was talking laconically into his radio. I couldn't look at any of them, only at what hung from the old swing frame in the playground, dangling between the disused swings that were slung over the crossbar by their chains.

At first I thought maybe it was a shop dummy someone had put there for a joke. Not a very funny joke, certainly, but it couldn't be real. And then I knew it was. The body hung motionless in the clear evening air, toes pointed downward like a ballet dancer, neck wrenched, tongue swollen and poking from its lips. That's all I made out, that and the placard hung round its neck that said: *NO SODEMY. JUSTISE FOR BISHOP TODD.*

'Turn round,' said Ming, gripping my shoulder. 'Walk. Don't run.'

I couldn't. Not for the life of me. Because pallid and distorted as the creature was, I recognised it now. *No*, not it. Him, him, *him*. Sallow skin turned ashen, and dark floppy hair. Dull eyes that had lost their hunted nervousness, lost everything. It was the boy from Ruth's gang, her protected henchman, her shadow.

Ming hauled at my shoulder. 'Go!'

My limbs wouldn't do anything by themselves so it was just as well he was ordering me around. That corpse terrified me. I could barely take my eyes off it. *HIM.*

'But we have to…'

'The police will come,' snarled Ming. 'We can't do anything, it's over. Don't look.'

It seemed a terrible inhuman thing to walk away, to *not look*. It seemed like abandoning the thing that hung there, abandoning the person it used to be, pretending it didn't exist and never had. I never exchanged one word with the boy. I never even knew his name, but I *knew* him.

I owed it to him to *look*. Was that rubbernecking? If it was, I understood the compulsion. 'But…'

'No.' Ming tried to frogmarch me back the way we'd come.

I found I was crying. I turned once more, and that's when Ming finally yelled at me.

'You always look back, don't you? You always have to look back!'

He was angry, but I couldn't be angry back because he was panicking, too. He began to run and I ran with him though my hip was starting to ache and smart worse than ever. His fingers were tight around my arm as if he was terrified of losing his hold, so I didn't complain. Glancing back, he dodged into a side street, hauling me on. I didn't understand why he was so afraid, though. Not till I heard the triumphant shout behind us, and Ming slid to a halt.

'Bugger,' said Ming.

Same word, same tone of voice, same old reason. Jeremiah Maclaren had turned the corner after us, his gang behind him. His gang had got bigger. Much bigger. That wasn't a gang any more, that was a mini-mob. I remembered, sick to my stomach, that despite his expensive education Jeremiah couldn't spell very well.

'Oy!' Jeremiah bellowed. 'You.'

Ming stood half-turned to him, holding me with both hands. His thumbs rubbed my arms, but I don't know if he was reassuring me or himself.

There was something different in the way the gang moved and breathed, something alien and bad. I didn't want Ming to get thumped again, and I didn't much want another beating myself, but it was more than that, it was scarier. You could taste something in the air, an invisible chemical that made your heart beat faster and your head spin with fear. It made me want to run again, and sod my poor old hip, but Ming just stood there. Perhaps he thought he could talk his way out of it.

'Jeremiah,' he said. He licked his lips. 'We're not looking for trouble.'

Jeremiah inched closer, his colleagues closing in at his back. I realised he was high, but he was high on something better than chemicals. His drug of choice: killing.

'You're always looking for trouble, Minger. You've got it now.'

'Don't do this, Jeremiah.'

Jeremiah smirked. 'Say please.'

Ming shrugged. 'Please don't do this.'

I wanted to meet his eyes, but I didn't dare take mine off Jeremiah. I thought if Ming let go of my arms I might fall, because my hip felt as if it didn't belong to me any more. *Don't do this to me!* I yelled inwardly at my stupid body. *Not right now! Now is not convenient!*

'See her?' said Jeremiah, nodding at me. 'Assaulted Rose Parsons. Rose is a good pious respectable kid, never harmed anyone, helps out in the soup kitchen at weekends. And this one half-strangled her. Broke her jaw.' He gave a hissing sigh of world-weary sorrow.

Despite his maudlin viciousness my heart leapt, because beyond the fidgeting mob I saw a police car slow and pause at the entrance to the side street. I waited for the creak and slam of a door, the sound of voices dispersing the sullen crowd, but it never came. I heard the engine noise purr louder, saw the white bodywork of the car slide away, and they were gone.

Jeremiah had watched my eyes, and now he smiled and turned his back on us – that's how confident he was – and addressed his acolytes like a regular little demagogue. 'She put poor Rose in hospital, and she only got off with it because her father's a cleric. A One Church Rector, yes, but he's a filthy hypocrite! A maggot in the belly of the Church. He has no faith. He's an unbeliever, an infidel, an *apostate!*'

I gasped as if he'd punched me in the gut. How did he know that?

'There's worse.' Jeremiah raised his hands, along with his voice. God, he was good. He must have been practising at home in front of his mirror. I couldn't see his face but I could imagine his holy solemnity. Bishop Todd could switch it on like a cheap lightbulb, after all, and Jeremiah was his faithful devotee.

When the muttering behind him died down, Jeremiah lowered his voice again, but you could hear it beautifully, every word, his voice expertly projected. 'That one,' he said, jerking his thumb at Ming. 'That unbeliever? His parents are dangerous subversives, plotters against the Church and the Mother of the Nation. I met him the day the Bishop vanished, begged him to tell me if he'd seen the holy man, and do you know what his answer was?'

Rumbling from the mob. 'What?' a voice shouted obligingly.

Wearily, Jeremiah shut his eyes and sighed. 'Laughter. Contemptuous laughter. That's how much this infidel cared for Bishop Todd.' He frowned thoughtfully, as if he was working something out in his head for the first time. 'Know what, though? He was coming from the countryside, the beautiful countryside where our Bishop loved to walk. He had scratches on his face, he was... *running*. And he was there...'

Jeremiah paused, gripped his head with his hands. For a long dramatic time he stayed like that, silent, as the atmosphere thickened with dread and hate.

When he snapped his head up very suddenly, his voice was a disbelieving hiss. 'It was the day he disappeared. The day. The Bishop. *Died*.'

Jeremiah Maclaren turned on his heel to look right at me and Ming. His followers couldn't see his face then, so they couldn't see the most evil smirk I've ever seen in my life.

Ming said, 'Run.'

I tried. Ming knew the streets, and that was the only reason they didn't catch us straight away, because Ming knew where to dodge and duck and squeeze round impossible corners. But I couldn't run fast, and I was breathless with terror and rage. Part of me wanted to go back and pound Jeremiah's jaw to a pulp. But it wasn't an option, and let's face it, my terror outweighed my temper by about fifty parts to one.

They were a powerful bunch of brutes, but unused to running. All they knew was how to string up defenceless boys, but enough rage was firing them to keep them on our heels. We kept ahead, just. Ming stumbled across the rubble of a demolition site, determinedly hanging on to me, and on that terrain we gained a good thirty metres of ground. They were too enraged to watch their feet, barging and shoving till they made one another stumble, but if they were clowns they were lethal ones.

Cover would delay them though; and there was cover. A block of flats had been sliced in half by the bulldozers, exposing old ghosts and forgotten lives to the air. You could see the outline of doors and walls and fireplaces, the shape of pictures that had hung in smoky rooms.

Ming yanked me into a doorway that used to be someone's bedroom door, judging by the scraps of floral wallpaper that hung limp in the windless air. A child had put up stickers that someone had tried to scrape off. SpongeBob Squarepants and Scooby Doo. Amazing what you notice.

The child was probably grown up by now. Maybe he was one of *them*. They hadn't seen our hiding place but they were fanning out, taking more care, shouting encouragement to one another as they hunted through the derelict buildings and the rubble-strewn alleyways.

Ming's breathing was a high-pitched sound in his throat. He swallowed and shut his eyes tight, forcing back his panic. At last he got his wind back, and his control, and put his arms round my shoulders and buried his face in my neck. Only for an instant, though. He pushed me away and jerked his head and said, 'You go that way.'

'What?' I looked where he was showing me, then back at him. 'No.'

'Yes. Please, please, Cass. Please don't argue. You can't outrun them. *Please*.' He stroked my face with his thumbs, almost crying. 'Please.'

I touched his face back. I didn't want to stop touching it. 'Okay.'

'See that tenement that's still intact? Make for that. Just run, run as hard as you can. There's a close running through to the main road. I'll head for the river, that way.'

I looked where he was pointing. 'I don't think you can get through…'

'Yes. Yes, I can. No problem. Meet me in the wood, usual place. Right?'

'Yes. Of course. Okay.'

'And Cass?' He held my face firmly and stared into it. 'This time don't look back.'

'No.'

'Promise me. This time. Do. *Not*. Look back. Swear it on…on my Pirate Orc Army of the Riverworld.'

'Yes. Okay.' I tried to smile at him. 'Yes. I promise, I swear.'

And that was it. No more time. He smiled back, then linked his fingers round mine and drew them down from his face.

'They're a good bit away. Down towards the sheds,' he whispered, glancing out. His knuckles were white where they gripped the sad old doorpost. 'There isn't going to be a better time. Run, Cassie. Run.'

• • •

I kept my promise. This time I did.

I did not look back, Ming, not even when I heard their shouts, heard them stumbling after me, hampered by the rubble. I had a bad hip, but I'd once been a Pirate Queen and God knew I could run over rocks better than anyone.

I didn't look back, so I don't know when you fell back. I don't know when they caught up with you. I don't even know if you did it deliberately, my fall guy one more time. One minute you were running, that's all I know, but you weren't running for the river like you'd said, you were running behind me, I don't know why. And the next I was running alone, pounding through the narrow bottleneck close, running even as I cried, knowing you weren't running any more, that they'd brought you down, knowing it from the tone of their howls.

Why didn't you run where you said? Why did you run at my back, slower than I knew you could run?

I don't know. Because maybe I was a coward but I'd sworn and I'd promised, the last promise I'd ever make you. I wouldn't look back, that's what I told you.

And this time I didn't.

21: Jetsam

It was stupid to go to Ming's house, but I couldn't think where else to go, and I'd been curled in a derelict shed on a patch of waste ground for ages, hugging my knees and wishing I could cry. I was completely numb, couldn't feel a thing, but there was a reason for that. My heart was lying in my chest in two pieces and I couldn't think how to put it back together.

So maybe my brain was in pieces too. Going back to Ming's house was an incredibly bad idea, but I couldn't face my family, and no way was I going to the police.

Besides, I'd promised Ming. I'd kept my promise about not looking back, and that was a good start. I was going to keep my other promise and meet him in the wood like he'd said, because if I was a good girl, if I never broke my word ever again, maybe Ming would be there. God would do this one thing for me since I hadn't asked for anything else in a long time. He might glower and stroke his beard and tap his fingers on his desk but he'd do this one thing for me because I was going to be good from now on, and I'd do anything, anything.

Being omniscient, God must know that, so he'd make sure the last hour never happened and Ming would meet me in the wood. No, no, *He'd* make sure of it. I had to start thinking of Him in capital letters again, if I was going to make any impression on the old Infinite Mercy.

Ming would expect me to rescue Keyser Soze, so though

Keyser Soze hated his pet carrier as much as he hated me, and my arms were covered in deep ragged gouges by the time I managed to heave the cage door shut, there was no way I was leaving him. Laying his ears flat on his head he hissed and rowled at me as I shoved random items into my backpack. They were all Ming's things. My stuff didn't matter, but I had to get this to Ming so he could get away. He'd need a toothbrush.

I stood for a moment, trying to think if I'd forgotten anything.

That's when the silence in the house became solid, weighing down on me like a sodden mattress. Terror clenched my throat, because it was so unexpected, that fear, so very out of place. I'd never been scared in Ming's house, never.

There was a sound. The click of a latch? The knock of a foot against a skirting board? Or only the tap of a branch against a window? But there was no wind out there. Perhaps a bird had brushed its wings against the glass.

It couldn't be ghosts. There were none here: all the ghosts were in the wood, where I should have gone at once. I knew that now, I knew I shouldn't have come here. My own heart was killing me, choking me with its insane clattering in my chest and throat.

I made myself creep down the stairs, one at a painful time. I even turned the corner at the landing with my eyes still open. I blinked at the downstairs hallway, and air rushed into my lungs in a single huge sob. Nothing there, nothing and no-one.

Almost out. Surely I'd imagined the creak of a hinge. There couldn't be anything lurking behind the sitting room door, and nothing could be crouching in the little gap under the stairwell. Just one more flight of stairs and please, please God, don't let my hip give out, don't let me fall, don't let me stumble and be at its mercy, whatever it is.

Let me out of here.

In the narrow hall I found I was crying, but that was just the pain in my hip. Everything else was *fine* because *Ming would be in the wood*. There was nothing to cry about. He'd said he'd meet me so he would; Ming never broke his word. The old artillery shell with the walking sticks was right by the door: I grabbed a stout ash stick as I paused, backpack over one shoulder and Keyser Soze spitting in his cage, then prised open the front door with an elbow. I could use the stick to beat Keyser Soze to death. Only joking.

I almost tumbled down the step in my rush to be out of there, and then I was out in the air, dizzy with relief. It was my imagination, that was all: my stupid fantastical mind inventing monsters when there were more than enough of those on the streets. I felt like a madwoman and I knew I must look like one, dusty from demolished homes, sweaty and dirty, crying with pain (and only pain), walking stick in one hand and cat in the other. I had a vague notion that people were crossing the street to get out of my way but that was fine with me. Really. A bag lady at fifteen. Wait till Ming saw me: he wouldn't stop laughing till I elbowed him in the diaphragm.

In the ghost wood I used the stick to swipe the webs aside, and I wasn't even afraid when spiders catapulted onto me. Ming wasn't here yet, or he'd come a different way; otherwise he'd have broken through already. That was okay. I'd wait for him. He'd be so proud of me when he knew I'd got through the spiders with no fuss at all. Keyser Soze had curled up in a big spitting ball of resentment, and I was trying not to swing him too much as I walked. Really, I was.

I walked right past our pine log. You might expect Ming to be there, but I knew he'd go further into the wood. Okay, I might have had a notion he'd meet me on the log, that he'd be sitting there grinning up at me through his untidy fringe, but as soon as I saw it, Mingless, I knew I'd been silly. Of course he'd go further in, down towards the river. That was where all our recent adventures had taken us. Besides, hadn't he asked me to swear on the Armies of Riverworld? That was a coded message. He'd meet me beside the river. Where we'd lain buck-naked in the summer sun, river water evaporating from our skin, his arm around me. Obviously.

I stumbled down the steep slope and dumped the walking stick on the rough ground, exclaiming with exasperation as I rubbed my hip. I hoped he was going to hurry up. I sat down in the grassy hollow. I sat and stared at the river, boiling and brown, the racket of it not lessening as the light did. I waited until the day dimmed and the trees blurred and the further edges of the wood faded into the twilight. I waited until all birdsong died, until Keyser Soze growled and grunted and fell asleep, a furball of hatred.

I waited until I knew at last that Ming wasn't coming. Then I began to cry.

• • •

An hour later I still didn't know what to do about Keyser Soze. I had some mad idea about releasing him into the wild, and I even started to hum *Born Free*, shakily and off-key, and fiddle with the catch of his pet carrier.

He slitted his amber eyes and curled back his lip to show his needle teeth. You daft cow, he said in my head. I'm not wild, I'm not even feral. But I'll be bloody cross if you dump me in a haunted forest to fend for myself. In fact I'll probably have you killed.

I sniffed, laughing and crying as I stuck one finger through the wire and poked at his scabby head in an effort to stroke it. You're all there is, I told him, I'd better keep you. And I'm all you've got, so you'd better be nice to me, gangster cat. You'll be wanting a liberal hand with the Kit-e-Kat Morsels.

A dry branch cracked behind me and I jerked my head round. It wasn't dark yet; the sky between the branches was unbleached denim, a nail trimming of moon hanging with Venus above me. For the first time since I'd entered the wood, it occurred to me to be afraid. Keyser Soze's threatening growl was silenced and he flicked one bitten ear back. Trying to stand up in his cage, he could only crouch on whatever a cat calls his hunkers. A brief breeze moved in the pine branches and was still. Another branch creaked, dry pine needles gave a breathy crunch under-foot, and I knew I was not alone in the wood.

I'd left the walking stick five yards back but I grabbed hold of the nearest boulder and used that to lever myself upright. I made myself stand and turn. Please God please God please God. Oh, please let me see greenish eyes through blond hair that needs cutting. Please let me see a flashing grin, even if half his teeth are missing. Please, God. By all the white hair on your chinny-chin-chin –

'Where did you put him?'

You know when you run water onto ice? That's how that voice cracked the silence.

'What did you do with him?'

'Who?' I could barely speak. As I took a step backwards, Keyser Soze extended a paw out of his cage to dig a nee-dlepoint claw into my ankle. I gasped in shock.

'You know who.'

I could barely see in the woody dusk, but I knew that voice.

'Tell me what you did with him,' said Jeremiah.

He was nothing but shadows and navy twilight, but I could see his movement, feel his breath contaminating the wood like death. He moved through the trees so that I had to turn, trembling, to keep track of him.

'Are you on your own?' I whispered.

'The others got bored.' There was a sneer in his silky hiss. I'm sure he meant it to be threatening, but it made him more human to me, and I breathed easier.

'Did you follow me?' I asked. I made sure to keep the fear in my voice.

'I thought you might go to the Minger's house.' He couldn't repress his supercilious pride. 'I waited there till you appeared, then I followed you here. I've been watch-ing you for ages, you know. Silly girl.'

'Aw. You're God's Special Forces, you.' I shut my eyes tight, then snapped them open. Stupid, stupid. Be afraid, I told myself. Be very afraid. It's the only language he un-derstands.

'Don't try to take the piss, Cassandra.'

'I'm not.' I sucked in a lungful of forest air to remind myself this was my territory, not his. 'You're on your own,' I said again.

'And? So?'

And. So. My brain was churning. Defragmenting. Hurry up, hurry up…bring me those files… 'You were on your own that other time too.'

'When?' He moved through the trees.

I turned again, keeping him in view. 'Ming got into a fight with you and you came off worst. That doesn't happen. You were on your own. Your friends weren't there.'

'You're taking the…'

'No, no. I swear I'm not.' *Please help me on this one, Jeremiah.* 'I'm only trying to…'

'Yeah, I met him that day. On the road up there,' said Jeremiah. 'By chance. Who says he beat me? Who says I came off worst? Little infidel shit.'

'What were you doing on the road? Why were you out in the…'

He lunged out of the trees with a speed and violence that knocked the breath from my lungs. I thought we'd both tumble back into the river, but grabbing my arms, Jeremiah yelled in my face. 'What did you do with him? I know it was you!'

'Who? Jeremiah, I…'

'*You know who!* You were in these woods, you and your Minger! *What did the pair of you do?*'

His mouth was flecked with spittle at the corners. I'd only seen that on old people. To be specific, I'd only seen it on Bunty when she was dying, her and her guilty conscience fading from the world. I stared at the corners of Jeremiah's lips, at his bared teeth, and I couldn't look away. I couldn't possibly look at his eyes.

'What were *you* doing here, Jeremiah?'

His greyish tongue came out to lick his lips, but it didn't shift the white flecks.

'Your mother should have rotted in jail,' he hissed at last. 'I saw what she did to Todd.'

'You saw.' I tugged free of his hands and backed off.

'Yes. I saw. The Eyes of Justice, Cassandra.'

Silence. Silence so heavy I couldn't take the weight of it. Something had to break it.

So I said, 'You finished him off.'

A breeze moved in the dusky skyward branches, a late blackbird fluted somewhere high and far. And Jeremiah laughed.

'Oh, yeah. I smote him! I smote that apostate in the name of the Lord!'

I put one foot behind the other, slowly, slowly backing off. 'Tell me. Tell me what happened.' My voice sounded mechanical. I was so afraid.

'I saw them. I drove past them up on the road, and they were arguing. Imagine, your mother berating a man like the Bishop! How dare she! I knew I had to protect him, but by the time I parked and ran back, they'd gone into the wood. I followed them, but I didn't show myself. The One God sent me, you see. It was God's will that I saw them that day. God sent me to watch over the Bishop.'

God was out to lunch, I thought, but I managed not to say it.

'They went so deep into the wood!' Jeremiah shook his

head. 'As if he was trying to get away from her, but she wouldn't leave him alone, the bitch. So I followed. I was as silent as an angel because I knew I might have to take her by surprise.'

I swallowed, over and over, because I knew how close he must have come to killing her. I wanted to be sick but I didn't dare. He might think I was possessed or something. I looked at his muscular arms, and gulped back the bile.

'Then they stopped, and I heard them,' he said dreamily. 'The river was loud, but the One God was with me and He made them raise their voices. I heard everything they said. You know, Cassandra, I worshipped Todd. *Worshipped* him. I wanted to be like him. No, I wanted to *be* him. And Todd betrayed me. He betrayed us all.'

'No,' I said. I shook my head violently, trying to keep up with the psychotic headcase. 'Todd stopped believing, that's all. He couldn't help that. They can't. When that happens they can't help it.'

'Heretic. Blasphemer. *Apostate.*'

'We – they don't want to stop believing,' I babbled. 'They don't want it to happen.'

Jeremiah's eyes were closed, his face raised to the deepening twilight sky. 'Can you imagine how angry I was? It wasn't the first time I'd followed Todd, you know. I wanted to be near him. I wanted to protect him. I wanted to *inhale* him. But I'd never heard him speak honestly before, can you believe it? *I* couldn't.' His brow furrowed. 'But that day? I heard what he said to your mother.' For a moment there was bewildered pain in Jeremiah's features, and tears in his eyes. He shrugged, and the humanity was gone.

'Then he turned his back on her, and she picked up a stone and hit him. She hit him *so hard!* Oh, she was angry. Not as angry as I was, Cassandra, but angry enough!'

I glanced quickly around me at the darkening wood. I couldn't see a single place to run to. Our cave was underwater, and even if it hadn't been, I couldn't have run there, not to a trap. I couldn't outrun this crazy boy. The rush and roar of the water wouldn't even let me think straight. I didn't know what I was going to do but I didn't want to die, that's all. And I knew what Jeremiah was going to do. He was going to kill me.

I stumbled back, my eyes on Jeremiah. He followed me, desperate to tell, hands open, face beseeching.

'Todd was just lying there, like some drunken sot. Insensible. A Bishop!'

I wanted to scream at him, *He wasn't drunk, you mad bugger! He was unconscious! What are you talking about?* The thing is, I don't think even Jeremiah knew what he was talking about. Not in real life.

'I watched over him till he started to come round, and he saw me. Perhaps he saw it in my eyes, Cassandra. The Light of the Avenging Angel, because he stumbled up and tried to run. But he was hurt, and he tripped and fell half in the river, and that was good, that was God's blessing on me, because there was so much blood. So much,' he whispered, 'but all in the river. The river turned to red wine. You see how many signs God gave me?'

'So you…'

'I hit him again, that's all. Just like your mother did, only I did it properly.' He sounded proud. 'It wasn't hard. Not once I got started.'

'My Mum didn't mean to...'

'Just like your mother!' he screamed again, drowning me out. 'Except she didn't strike him down for a holy purpose. She wasn't like me! She struck him out of venal self-interest! Oh, she should have rotted in jail. Her and your apostate father!'

I swallowed, but my throat wouldn't close. I can't describe how scared I was then.

'She *would* have rotted in jail,' he went on casually, 'if it hadn't been for you. See, I panicked to begin with. I ran away, I wasn't thinking straight. But on the next Sunday, it came to me like a revelation. I realised at last what God intended. I loved Bishop Todd, you see; it was your mother who led him to his death. It was *your mother* who should be punished. So I knew then. I knew I must come back to the wood, find the body, and call for help. I must lead God's forces of justice to the Bishop. But when I came back, he was gone!'

I breathed carefully, in and out. In and out.

'You hid that body, didn't you? You, Cassandra, you and the Minger. You must have, you're the only ones who come near this wood, you're the only ones who'd do such a thing. What did you do with Todd? You must have been quite clever. Where did you put the Bishop, Cassandra? Not in the river. He'd have washed up long before now.'

'You killed him,' I said, stunned, 'and you'd have let my Mum hang for it.'

I might as well have said not a word. 'You haven't paid for that yet, Cassandra. Hiding Todd, keeping his body from the people who loved him.' Jeremiah's eyes were misty again. 'You haven't paid for that terrible deed, and neither has the Minger. Where is he?'

'You're mad,' I said clearly. 'You're mad. You *know* where Todd is. He washed up on the beach north of the harbour. Maybe he was caught underwater for a while, ever thought of that?' Not strictly a lie, I thought, mentally crossing myself.

'What did you do with him?' He was all strained tolerance. 'Where did you hide him?'

'Jeremiah.' I knew I was talking for my life. 'We. Have just. Had. This conversation. I'm not hiding Todd.' *Not now, anyway.* 'He's in the morgue, Jeremiah. Okay? Listen, why don't we go there now? I'll come with you. You were very fond of Todd, weren't you? That's okay. You're upset and I…'

'You're taking the mickey again, Cassandra.' His voice turned cold and crystal-clear. 'Who gives a flying toss for that apostate? Of course I know where *he* is, now. Todd's rotting in Hell. Now I'll ask again: where is he?'

'I don't understand!' I screamed. '*I don't understand!*'

'For the last time,' said Jeremiah patiently, 'where did you put your infidel lover?'

'What?' I said stupidly.

'The Minger. Where are you hiding him?' He lunged forward to grab my arms again.

God. Oh, God. I felt the most violent impulse I've ever felt in my life, and I could barely get a grip on myself. But I had to, because I had to know. 'I'm not hiding him,' I said, my voice small and frightened and shaking like a bike going over cobbles. I had to keep it that way.

He shook me like a doll. 'We've got rope now, Cassandra,' he leered. 'If we'd had one then, he'd be swinging from a lamp post already, and the police wouldn't dream of touching us. Shame we'd used all our rope on the sodomite.' He sighed. 'Shouldn't have left the Minger lying there, I suppose. That was a mistake, but we knew he wouldn't be moving. He couldn't have. Not by himself.'

I stayed absolutely silent. Bile was back in my throat, and revulsion. I couldn't speak but I kept thinking, Tell me, go on. Go on and tell me, please. Please. Jeremiah was my little god at that moment, my awful, unholy, all-knowing god. The hope was frail and feeble but it was hope. He had to tell me. Oh, please.

'I mean, we left him for dead. He probably was. Did you even recognise him? Are you sure you got the right guy?' He gave me a cruel smile. 'Who helped you? You couldn't have moved him by yourself, Cripple, and you couldn't have gone far. He's not at his house, I'd searched it before you got there, so where did you take him?'

I smiled then. I just couldn't help myself, but it was a bad move. I put my hands over my mouth to hide my giant grin but it was too late, and anyway, he could still see the smile in my eyes. Jeremiah's face darkened and swelled, puffy with hatred.

'We'll find him, *Cassandra*.' He made my name a mockery. 'When we do we'll string him up anyway. You haven't saved him. And I do believe we'll string you up with him!'

I don't know what he meant to do when he yanked me against him. Just snarl his hate in my face, maybe, but that wasn't what my reflexes thought. They went berserk all by themselves.

As I thrashed and lashed at him he snatched my throat,

jerked and shoved. Catching a glimpse of his face, dark brown eyes out on stalks with panic and hatred, I thought, he's like a spider. Calm down. *He's more scared of you than you are of him. He's more scared of you…*

My overworked hip picked that moment to give out on me at last. It went from under me and I collapsed, and Jeremiah, taken by surprise, fell with me, his one-handed grip on my throat slipping. As I rolled aside I kicked and bit, hammering at him with my fists and my working foot. And with every yowl and recoil of his, with every chance I got when he was off me even for a moment, I was scrabbling around on the ground.

At the risk of repeating myself: rocks are never around when you need one. I was sobbing and gasping with terror before my hand closed around something solid and smooth: Ming's dad's walking stick. Whatever. It would have to do. Grabbing it with two hands I rolled and swung it into the side of Jeremiah's head as he came at me. As he stumbled back, I hit him again, and staggered to my feet through the agony in my hip, and hit him again.

After that it would be easy to say it wasn't me doing it, it was my mother with a rock, it was Bunty with a rolling pin. But it was me, it was all me, no excuses. I beat him back, his hands alternately shielding his bloody face and snatching viciously at me. When he was teetering on the edge of the crumbling slope where the river was eating its own banks, he pulled his hands away from his face and clenched them into fists, glaring at me in shock and pain and rage.

It was the rage that did for him, because watching him spit fury along with his fear, I knew for certain it was him or me. It was him or Ming. And of course, it was him or Griffin. Because I knew fine who must have dragged Ming away from his lynching, and it wasn't me.

'You godless witch!' screamed Jeremiah.

As he lunged at me, the fragile riverbank went from under him and he stumbled. Taking my only chance, I swung the ash stick hard. It caught him on the side of the neck, and Jeremiah went down like a shot bird, tumbling and plunging into the murky racing flood.

It flung and rolled him, and as he caught on a submerged rock the water mountained up against him. For a ghastly age he stuck there, drifting, battered as a piece of weed, head hanging back and swinging with the wild current, eyes bulbous and looking straight at me. Did he blink? I don't know, but I realised then that his eyes had always looked dead. The next second, the river tore him free and swallowed him.

I stared and stared into the gathering darkness, till even the far bank and the trees had merged with the dusk, and the dusk had merged with the night, and all that marked the river's presence was its awful torrential sound.

My eyes stung and ached with staring, and I breathed mechanically, over and over, forcing myself to do it. That was all I could do. Only when I knew for sure that Jeremiah wouldn't be crawling out again did I let myself start to cry.

• • •

I don't know if Jeremiah was dead when he went into the water. I don't know if I broke his neck first, and I'll never know. They'd have been able to tell, I think, but they never did find Jeremiah Maclaren. Not all bodies wash up.

Not all secrets, either.

After

Dearest Cass,

I hunted all over town for you, you misbegotten trollop. Why did you guys sneak off without me? That day of all days. Hadn't you watched the news? And if you and that idiot weren't always trying to dodge me, I might have got there earlier.

Come to think of it, that might not have helped. I didn't think for a minute you'd go back to his house. Didn't you realise? The cops would have taken the keys off his parents and that means the militias would have got copies too. What possessed you? Anything could have happened, and you're lucky nothing did. I wouldn't have dreamed of looking for you there, and anyway, I couldn't do everything, could I? Do you have any idea how hard it is dragging a bloody corpse into hiding without being seen? I wish I'd thought of calling Wilf earlier, but that's what sheer panic does to you.

When I did phone him, Wilf showed within five minutes. Driving a hearse, can you believe it? A hearse! God knows where he got it. Knowing Wilf's hotline to the Almighty, God probably provided it. Of course we put poor Ming in the coffin. I'm ashamed to tell you, Cass, I know it's horrible and inappropriate and you'll be hurt, but I want to tell you everything about that journey. I laughed *and laughed. I laughed almost all the way to the border. When I started crying Wilf stopped the car and slapped my face and bought me some whisky. But we were over the border by then.*

Please try and write again. Please give me the news. I'm sorry it's taken me so long to write back but it took your letter ages to find me. I want you to keep me up to date – for once. And you know what I mean and don't pretend you don't.

You didn't tell me. What news of Abby?

Folding Griff's letter, I eased it back into its envelope. I didn't want to tear it or crease it. It hadn't gone through the regular post, of course, but hand to hand through friends, and I didn't know when I'd get another. Anyway, I didn't know how many times I was going to have to read it and re-read it before I got up the courage to answer it. I knew I could lie. I could lie beautifully; it runs in the family. But I didn't think I could lie to Griff, tell him Abby got community service, tell him she was slogging her guts out down the Laundries. Like I wished she was.

A month after that terrible day with Jeremiah, I came home and found Mum staring silently into the cooker hood and Dad leaning his head on the table, his hands clasped behind his neck. As if he was thinking about praying but couldn't quite remember how it was done.

I'd told them about Ming, obviously. And we knew that it was because of what happened to him that Griff disappeared that day, too. But I could never tell them what happened to Jeremiah. They couldn't know that, not ever. To paraphrase what Mum told Dad a hundred years ago:

what your parents don't know about you, they can't let slip. Best not to know. I knew we'd spend our lives keeping secrets now, trying desperately to protect each other, but maybe that wasn't such a bad thing. Maybe that was normal even when the world was normal, too.

The world wasn't normal that day. I saw their faces and said, 'What is it?'

'It's Abby,' said Dad. Beside the cooker Mum had started to cry, silent sobs convulsing her thin body.

'What?' I couldn't even be afraid at that point. I didn't have any space left for extra terror. 'Have they charged her? What is it? Is she still in jail?'

'It's worse than that,' said Dad. 'They let her go.'

A low keening sound came out of Mum and just went on, endlessly, levelly, as if there came a point when misery heaped on misery couldn't get any heavier.

'What?' I didn't understand.

Dad hauled his head off the table and looked into my eyes and said, 'You have to leave.'

And now I understood him fine.

• • •

We never saw Abby again. They'd released her without warning: they didn't tell her lawyer, they didn't tell Mum and Dad, they didn't even tell her, till the last moment. They just took her out of her cell and gave her back her belongings and let her go. Maybe they laughed and told her to make a dash for it. Maybe she did run. I don't know how far she got before the militia caught up with her. I'll never know, because they never even gave us back her body.

• • •

We saw Ma Baxter on TV here, Cass. Looked mad as hell, still banging on desperately about Dark Forces though they can't prove it was murder. No wonder she's angry. The fun she could have had! I suppose Todd was in quite a state by the time he washed up. The experts on the news here said he was so damaged and decayed they couldn't tell how he died, and that head wound could have been post mortem, and even Ma B had had to admit it.

The only problem with that, sister dear, is that if he fell in all by himself it would prove there's a God. So perhaps it was the ghosts in the wood. Perhaps they enticed him in there in the first place. I always liked them.

Okay, I believe you didn't kill him. I know that now. But can you imagine what I thought when I found that thing in the cave? I nearly came straight home and throttled you, but I know why you and Ming did what you did. And you were right. They would have blamed Dad. It all worked out for the best.

Dark forces, that's you.

I'm fine. I like it here. I'm eating now, honest. They treat refugees a bit like beggars and thieves, but Ming's cousin reckons he can get me on a teacher training course, once I get my Immigrant status formalised. They need teachers, apparently. You can tell Mum that. And tell her So There. And give her a kiss for me while you're at it. I miss her. I miss you all.

Cass, what happened with you, after that terrible business with the mob? How did you get home that day, after you went to Ming's? I'm sorry I wasn't there to help you. You say Jeremiah hasn't been seen since, but watch yourself. Watch your back. Please.

I hope he fell in the river too, though. You never know. Maybe there is a God.

• • •

You see how I tell nobody anything? It's better for them and it's better for me. I folded Griff's letter and unfolded it, then did all that all over again. Stupid. If I kept mauling it like this, it would disintegrate. It was just that I couldn't leave it alone.

I laid it carefully on my bedside table, smoothed down its smudged envelope. Once more I looked around the room, trying to think what I'd regret leaving. There wasn't much space in the backpack but I'd hate to leave something really important. Apart from my mother and my father, that is, and my friends, and my whole life. You couldn't fit all that in the bag I'd been allowed.

Wilf was adamant. *You're supposed to be coming with me for work experience. It's a conference and there's only two overnights. For God's sake, Cassandra, you don't need to take the sodding kitchen sink. How would that look?*

He didn't use the word 'sodding', by the way. Wilfred Makunga has some mouth on him, for a One Church rector, but I guess his nerves are shot. That's hardly surprising.

He ferries rebels. He doesn't agree with them but he ferries them out anyway. Easy because he's beyond reproach. So far.

He's ever so high in the One Church: Bishop-elect. It's one reason I'm not so scared of leaving Dad here, but oh, Wilf will have so far to fall, should anyone decide to push him.

I can't worry about Wilf, though. I can't think about anyone but myself, my family. I can't even dwell for more than a moment on Ruth, Ruth who finally convinced me I had to go, that Dad was right and I had to leave. Not that she ever spoke to me again. The day we went back to school I looked for her, but I didn't see her, not for ages. That was because I didn't recognise her and when I finally did, she turned her back on me.

Who knows why? Pride, shame, humiliation, rage? Maybe a combination. Her hair all roughly sheared off, her bruised face stripped of makeup, her shoulders hunched in defeat, her fingers shuddering with a tremor that never stopped. I heard the militias caught up with her and taught her a little humility. One lesson was all it took. She's no rebel any more. She's alone; her gang deserted her for their own good, and of course her loyal silent shadow is gone forever. How she must miss him. I miss her, but I can't think about Ruth.

But before I saw her, I argued. I argued with Dad a lot.

'You're going,' he said. 'Wilf will take you and you're bloody lucky. Who's to know who'll be last out? Take your chance while you've got it.'

'I don't want to leave you,' I cried.

'You're going,' he said again. 'I can't go on being this afraid for you. I'll disintegrate. I'm so afraid for you, Cass, and I'm so afraid for the future, what's waiting for you here. It's getting worse, can't you see that? You're a girl. You're my smart girl. You can see that.'

I couldn't see anything past my tears.

He watched my eyes, watched them wander round the room and come to rest on Keyser Soze, on all I had left of Ming. I felt rotten about it but I still hated that animal.

'We'll keep the cat,' he said. Tried to smile and didn't make it.

'Come too,' I begged. 'You and Mum. Why not?'

'Cass,' he said. He swallowed. 'I hear him calling, Cass. I can hear him yell my name.'

'Him,' I echoed. 'Him with a capital H.'

'Him. It's like He's yelling from behind a brick wall but He's there, He's somebody I thought was dead and I can't leave till I find Him.'

I wanted to shout, *What about me! Why am I less important than your God? I need you too, and I'm not hiding.*

But I didn't say it. It wasn't his God, of course, calling plaintively like some lover who's gone too far with playing-hard-to-get and wants some attention again. It wasn't Him, it was Dad's own desperation, or his own younger surer self. And for Dad's self-delusion I almost hated him.

But maybe, just maybe, it was his God. In which case he'd better stick around waiting for a bit. And after all, Dad was sending me away, and that meant I was important to him too. Maybe almost as important as *Him*.

I'd had my idols, after all, my own smaller gods. I'd lied to Dad too. I'd done my own betraying.

• • •

I'm glad your period came, Cassandra, but that is Way Too Much Information. I'm just relieved I don't have to do the Honour Killing thing with Ming, just as he's getting better.

The corpse sends his love. He got fed up yesterday, so we yanked out his remaining monitors and checked him out. Oh, and he did not flirt with any nurses. He told me to write that. Make of it what you will. He can write and explain himself when his arms are working again. I better tell you, he's ugly, but not half as ugly as he deserves to be. Missing an eye, but he says you'll like the pirate look. Anyway, I dare say he'll be gorgeous again in about a year. He's making the most of his invalidity. Jeez, he owes me. He'll be making toast for me for a year when he's better.

He sends his love. Again. All of it. Do I have to write this stuff? I'll throw up on the laptop. Anyway, he never shuts up about you. When are you coming, he says? I know you said no more promises, but just to get some peace I told him soon, really soon. So I'm glad you're on your way.

It's better here for us, that's the thing. For now, anyway. I know we'll all go home one day, Cass. I know it.

I send my love too. Do up your buttons, you trollop.

Love & kisses

Griff   xxxxxxxxxx

I stroked my brother's letter, and tucked it carefully into the front pocket of my backpack, where I could reach it very easily. Then I drew it out again, once more, just to read the…

P.S. Ming says Keyser Soze sounds happy and settled, seeing as he's taken over your house. He says give him a hug before you leave him.

I said I'd write that, but between you and me, Cassandra? It'll be fine by me if you don't.

The End